perfect pitch

perfect pitch

1) home ground

EDITED BY
SIMON KUPER

review

First published in softback in 1997
by HEADLINE BOOK PUBLISHING

A REVIEW softback

10 9 8 7 6 5 4 3 2 1

ISBN 0 7472 7698 6

Typeset by
Letterpart Limited, Reigate, Surrey
Printed and bound in Great Britain by
Mackays of Chatham PLC, Chatham, Kent

HEADLINE BOOK PUBLISHING
A division of Hodder Headline PLC
338 Euston Road
London NW1 3BH

contents

acknowledgements

Thanks to Sophie Breese, Tomaso Capuano, Robert Chote, Ben Simonds-Gooding, Simon Luke, Annalena McAfee, Marcela Mora y Araujo, Matthijs van Nieuwkerk, Nick Royle, Vivienne Schuster, Henk Spaan, Robert Walpole, Tom Watt and Alexander Wolff, and to Ian Marshall and Geraldine Cooke at Headline.

Submissions to *Perfect Pitch* are welcome. These should be accompanied by a stamped, self addressed envelope and sent to: Simon Kuper, c/o *Perfect Pitch*, Headline, 338 Euston Road, London NW1 3BH.

perfect pitch

The idea came from Holland. *Hard Gras* (the name means what you think it does) began life three years ago as a kind of literary magazine solely devoted to football. With its mix of fiction, poetry and non-fiction, every issue has reached the Dutch bestseller lists. The magazine is the source of Hugo Borst's marvellous story about the Van Basten family, which you can find in this issue of *Perfect Pitch*.

Surely, we thought, there was room for a *Hard Gras* in England? Most people here accept that it is possible to write well about football. Yet, as D.J. Taylor remarks in this issue, the game is still 'crying out to have novels written about it'.

And much of the football non-fiction of recent years has consisted of failed attempts to copy Nick Hornby. 'I stood on the terraces at Hartlepool for years and we always lost and it rained', that sort of thing. In Taylor's words, that's meagre for a sport 'central to the upbringing of about half the UK's adult male population'. Not to mention that of a growing number of females.

Perfect Pitch hopes to fill the gap, with writing by novelists, poets, journalists and sometimes even by footballers – preferably ones like Jorge Valdano, who have scored in a World Cup final.

This issue is loosely based around the 'Home Ground' theme. Issue two appears next spring.

Simon Kuper, editor

dying with diego

JIMMY BURNS

This is a story about two stories, or rather, about two stories that became one, thanks to my encounters with a tragic genius in the world of professional football.

It's about what Diego Maradona said and did once my (unauthorised) biography of him, *Hand of God*, was published; and the strange transformation that began to take place in my life as a result of writing about Diego Maradona. Along the way we each took a little bit of the other.

I blame Diego for wanting to get this story going by choosing to come to London in early September 1996 just as my book is beginning to find its way into the bookshops. Following a steady decline into drug-induced neurosis, Diego has temporarily rediscovered his zest for life just as I am sinking into a monumental state of depressed inactivity as a result of a woman I have known deciding she has had enough of me.

I know I am not the first man in the world to have this happen to him but, dear reader, I hope you will sympathise with my dilemma. The woman in question is a highly gifted sports journalist whose Dad took her to her first game at the age of seven and who now knows more about football than I will ever do.

For over a year I have been sharing each inner thought and phrase with this woman as the book takes shape, learning more about Diego through her eyes, and about myself. I begin to see Diego much as Sancho saw Quixoté – a bit of a nutcase but a dreamer nonetheless. I remember one day when she had just read a draft chapter and said: 'I know how your moods change as you write the book.'

Francisco Franco's unauthorised biographer, the English historian Paul Preston, remarked once how difficult it had been – while researching and writing – to put up in his home with an uncongenial uninvited guest in the person of the old dictator. My woman friend has no love lost for Maradona and somehow, I feel, begins to confuse me with him. On the day the book is published she says she'd had enough with a suddenness and mystery that used to characterise Maradona's better goals. Excuse the analogy but then that's what mixing love with football does to one.

'But you've written the book. You should feel good about that,' she says, in a moment of last-minute tenderness perhaps inspired by her own guilt.

'What's the point of the book without you?' I plead, thinking momentarily on the Thames and what a good place for a suicide. She has no answer.

Soon after that, someone rings me from Buenos Aires on the eve of Diego's arrival in the English capital to play me back a recording of a radio interview he has given. It is an upbeat Diego I am listening to. He and his wife Claudia are having another go at having their first son: 'I hope my sperm can get in there this time,' Diego tells a young Argentine reporter as they share pasta and a tomato salad in his flat. A few weeks earlier he had quit Boca Juniors amid fresh public admissions of his drug problem and after missing several penalties. I may not score goals the way I used to, he seems to be telling us, but I can still fuck and procreate.

In 1986, during that game with England, Maradona thanked God for his first hand ball. When he missed the penalties for Boca, Maradona blamed it on hell. 'It's the witches. They are against me,' he tells the local media. I guess I'm living under a kind of spell too, not a brilliant one. My star has fallen out of the sky, gone splat. I was brought up by the Jesuits, but not even they prepared me for Diego.

Just when I thought I had seen the end of him, crafted the final chapter, Diego announces he is coming to London as the star guest of an international football festival of school children sponsored by Eurosport and Puma. The English might still remember him for cheating them with his hand, but he speaks only fondly of them. After all, about this time, a year previously, he was enthusiastically received at Oxford University and given the honorary title of Inspirer of Dreams.

But I'm not only depressed, I'm also paranoid. I don't believe Diego's coming to London simply to kick a ball around in Battersea Park with a bunch of kids. Soon after the radio interview, I wake up in the middle of the night covered in sweat: a panic attack follows a nightmare about Diego chasing me round Trafalgar Square with an army of lawyers in pin-stripes and bodyguards carrying violin cases. To make matters worse I also dream about my woman friend befriending somebody else. He is another sports writer who I found with her after watching England play Switzerland in Euro 96. I was drunk at the time – had to be – because I threatened to kill him.

By then nearly a year had gone by since I first appeared on Argentina's most popular TV chat show alongside Diego's manager Guillermo Coppola and the former Argentine coach Carlos Bilardo and announced that I was preparing a book about the life and times of Maradona. That flippant boast I now imagine has come back to haunt me. Diego is on his way to London, as they say in cockney slang, to 'rearrange my furniture' – to beat me up in other words, mentally, physically, and legally.

Then I remember some old advice from my late Spanish grandmother: the best way to deal with a striker is to strike first. With two aggressive women friends (not the one I've been telling you about) for bodyguards and armed with a copy of my book, I make my way late on a Saturday night to San Lorenzo, near Harrods in Knightsbridge, where I've been tipped off Diego is having supper.

Unless you're a journalist or happen to have written a book about Diego Maradona, San Lorenzo is the kind of place you can get into only if you've got money or you've got a title. Eric Clapton likes it. So does Princess Di. Diego goes there to show that there is nowhere in the world that should be barred to him. He may not be an aristocrat, but he left the poverty of the shanty town behind him long ago.

Diego is sitting at the table with Coppola, his personal trainer, and Vialli. The Italian Chelsea player is silent and sober (he's got a match to play at Stamford Bridge the next day), but Diego's been drinking and who knows what else to help him along. He seems unable to focus on me or what any of us are doing there. He doesn't even seem to remember that we've been together before and that I've been following him all the way from Buenos Aires to Oxford via Naples, Barcelona and Paris, and that I've written a book about him.

I realise that it's the kind of state of mind that can lead to everything – a smashing of a glass, a broken bottle over the head, tables turning – or nothing at all. I hand him the book as one who hands his opponent a pistol in a game of Russian roulette. I would like to believe that I am handing him part of his soul. Scribbled into the inside cover is the dedication: 'To Diego, with a human sense of life.' What I mean is that I believe my biography to be critical but truthful. But then as Ossie Ardiles, speaking of Maradona, once told me: 'The truth hurts.'

Diego takes the book much as he had earlier taken the menu, overlooking the dedication, and flipping through its pages with the air of someone who hasn't got the stomach or the mindset here and now to get back into his soul. He pauses only to look at the photographs, chuckling like a naughty boy at one in particular – him posing with the Giuliano family (head of the Naples Camorra) in 1986.

If I too have said nothing until this moment, other than 'Here Diego, this is the book I've written about you!' – it's because my fear has given way to a form of fascination, as I wait for Diego's reaction. Diego continues to say nothing to me which is when I realise that he may be seeing me clearer than I had thought possible at first, and that he is not about to thank me or hit me but rather just ignore me.

He has taken the pistol, and shot, but he is alive and well and dining in San Lorenzo. As he closes the book and pushes it across the table at Coppola, a group of waiters come up and ask for his autograph in Italian. They are followed by the owner of the restaurant who embraces Diego like a long-lost brother. The whole restaurant now seems to be focused entirely on him. Somehow San Lorenzo takes on the aspect of a film set for *The Godfather*, with Italians kissing each other in a ritual of tribal complicity.

'You son of a bitch, Diego,' I think to myself. 'I've bust my ass trying to find out in a year what you've been hiding for most of your life and you haven't got a word to say to me.'

In the whole restaurant this night, only one table looks on the whole scene not with adoration but with cool detachment verging on amusement. The men and women on this table are blue blood English, have gone to private school and inherited great wealth. They go shooting and hunting and play polo. They gave up shopping in Harrods the day it was bought by an Arab, but somehow San Lorenzo remains part of their social circuit. Tonight their territory is close to being invaded and they realise just how close when one of the women gets up to go to the toilet. She is tall and blonde and with the rose skin of the pampered English female – a kind of Lady Di look-alike. Diego gets half off his chair and speaking loudly and in Spanish asks her to join his table. Her boyfriend gets up and half aggressively says in English: 'Excuse me, Mr Maradona, but she is my fiancée, and she already has a table.'

And Diego bursts out laughing as the woman goes on walking past, and the waiters laugh with him, and he apologises in a way he knows no one will believe, least alone me. At that moment I hate and love Diego Maradona.

I may be nursing an obsessive melancholy still, but Diego at least makes it clear that this is not to be a night of revelations. We could have sat through it, drinking and maybe snorting coke together, going over each other's lives, but instead Coppola stops me from joining them in the taxi that takes them from San Lorenzo to the Ministry of Sound nightclub then back to the Dorchester Hotel, where the whores sometimes mix with the rich.

'You know Diego's not happy with that Englishman,' Coppola whispers menacingly to one of my girlfriends, pointing to me. I realise then the roulette is just beginning.

According to the *News of the World*, Diego, after San Lorenzo, arranges for several ladies of the night to join him back at the hotel. He picks on a Brazilian and snorts cocaine with her. I've no firm evidence that the newspaper's story is accurate, but I guess anything is possible in London's Mayfair in the early hours of a Sunday morning. I go to bed that night with a part of me nursing a strange kind of envy. Without my woman friend I feel as abandoned in this city as a dog without his lead.

Then things start looking up for me just as they have been doing for Diego. Next day, while Diego is followed round Battersea Park by hundreds of adoring fans, I get a phone call from a TV station in Madrid inviting me to appear on their highest rated programme. It is just the escape I'm looking for.

With the onset of English winter I suffer easily from light denial syndrome, and I need the warmth and light of Spain where I was born eight years before Diego.

But then he and I are beginning to follow each other like body and shadow as I discover when, four days later, I fly into Madrid. Diego has flown from London to Alicante in southern Spain to submit himself to yet another drugs cure, as always administered by a specialist few other doctors have ever heard of. Diego believes in medicine men not the medical profession, in miracles and divine inspiration, and cheating life and death. It's September, a time when top footballers around Europe are cashing in on their latest massive transfer deals and engaging their talents in a new season. But in Alicante, Diego Maradona, the person once widely acclaimed as the greatest footballer of them all, mounts a scene which, had it been Chicago, might have been scripted by Norman Mailer.

It is Mailer who in his book *The Prisoner of Sex* has this to say about the price of fame: 'Fame is your phone ringing a few times more each week to request interviews you do not wish to give and don't, fame is people with kindly intentions interrupting your thoughts on the street, fame is the inhibition which keeps you from taking a piss in a strange alley for fear of cops and headlines on the dance floor. Fame is the inability to get boozed anonymously in a strange bar, which means it is the inability to nurse an obsessive melancholy through a night of revelations.'

Sure, I'm learning something about fame with Diego. In Alicante he pours out his latest confession about his drug addiction in a local radio interview before slamming my book as a crucifixion. 'Burns is really out of order, he's pissed all over me,' he declares before naming a list of players, managers and agents he threatens to take legal action against for the help they gave me in researching his life story. I hear later that of course he has not read the book because he speaks no English.

However his personal trainer, who does, reads him the first couple of pages which are full of acknowledgements. Diego feels betrayed and claims that his friends are now enemies.

A few hours later he returns to his hotel and tells Coppola he wants to hit the night, starting off in a local nightclub which doubles up as a brothel. Coppola tries to restrain him at first but then, as managers have done throughout Maradona's career, gives in, lets him go, a necessary indulgence for he who is beyond good or evil, a demi-god of the sporting world. Diego arrives at the nightclub, spots some male clients talking to some women and gets the owner to pay them off – the men that is.

In the early hours of the next morning, Diego returns to his hotel a second time, this time in a state of mind a bellboy describes as 'very strange and exalted'. Together with two women, Maradona gets stuck in the lift when the electrics fail. I suffer from claustrophobia and panic attacks too, so I can understand something of what Diego now feels, but what happens next suggests the extent to which our separate existences have yet to fully coincide.

For Maradona the lift experience is not just a bit of temporary anxiety. It becomes a bad trip into hell and back, a feeling that has haunted him before, a suffocating sense of entrapment, of dreadful darkness, of inability to escape, like when, as a child, he falls into an open sewer of the shanty town and starts drowning in the communal shit before being rescued by his Uncle Cirilo. Now in Alicante, Diego lashes out with the frenzy of an animal brought in from a wild landscape and dumped in a sealed cage. In that scene in the lift, with Diego kicking until his foot bleeds and his body bathed in sweat, there is projected the enemy he has always carried without and within himself.

Afterwards, the hotel manager will find the consequences of Maradona's rage which erupts once Diego is rescued by the local fire brigade. He kicks and hits everything he sees, breaks tables and chairs, cries into the night. 'Your work is a pile of shit,' he screams at the man from the insurance company who has come to assess the damage.

Alicante occurs exactly a year after Maradona returned in triumph to play for his old club Boca Juniors having served a 15-month ban for failing a World Cup dope test in the US. There is a sense of *déjà vu*. Maradona's life has been like a helter-skelter, oscillating between stardom and disgrace. Those of us who have followed his career through the years are as wary about declaring him finished as we are of proclaiming his enduring success. And yet even close friends of Maradona are whispering in private what they are afraid to say in public: if Diego goes on like this, he's going to die soon.

I'm thinking on Diego as I sit on a chair having my face painted with eye shadow and blush in preparation for my live TV appearance. The pressures of fame, the distortions and disruptions to life that money makes . . . The TV programme is Spain's most popular, which is to say that I have made a pact with the devil. In return for a free return ticket to Madrid, and the chance to promote my book in Spain, I have agreed to appear in a programme that sandwiches serious reportage between crude comedy and soft porn.

In the waiting room I sit for a while with the other invited guest. Her name is Lucia, a Catalan girl in her late twenties who looks and speaks as if she had it tough. 'I'm here because I've been abusing my body since the age of ten,' Lucia says to me lifting her skirt and showing me two large burn marks on her thighs. Her wrists are scarred from an earlier attempt to experiment with profuse bleeding.

Lucia tells me she was abused as a child, and has been raped five times since puberty, the last time in the mental asylum near

Barcelona from which she has escaped to appear on the programme.

'I do have another life you know,' she confides as the minutes tick away towards deadline. 'I like writing, particularly poetry. I guess it's my way of trying to discover love.'

I appear first on the programme. I find myself having to use twenty years of journalistic experience to anticipate and control an interview clearly set on bringing out only the most negative points about Diego.

Although I would not claim to see Diego yet as my best friend, I do try to paint a sympathetic picture of a victim of people who should know better than to wreck people's lives: so-called doctors and managers and politicians who have exploited Maradona in the course of his career. The interviewer wants me to deliver the final 'estocada' or sword thrust to a genius who may be mortally wounded, but I wind up the interview on a note of reconciliation.

'It's a pity Diego has lashed out at the book without reading it. We could have sat round and had a drink instead,' I say before the cameras move to Lucia.

Poor Lucia. No journalistic training there. Just a raw pathetic victim of life, pictures of her brutalised nakedness flashed across millions of TV screens as she tries to explain why she does what she does.

That night Lucia and I find ourselves being put up, at the TV company's expense, in the same luxury hotel in central Madrid. The concierge thinks I've brought her in from the streets and gives me a conspiratorial look as we ask for separate keys. Then, just as we are about to enter the lift, I turn to Lucia and ask if she'd like to come out with me for a late-night drink. 'There is nothing I feel like more,' Lucy says, all the tension of a ruined life somehow temporarily giving way to a totally innocent smile.

★ ★ ★

Diego returns to Buenos Aires, and I to London. Diego carries on with his drug cure – it seems eternal, this dealing with witches, trying to come to terms with getting older, never playing football the way he once did.

I feel we're struggling together – Diego and I – now that my dad's died and the book's written and there's a single postcard of some Vietnamese peasant sitting on my desk with the unsigned handwritten inscription 'Miss Saigon'. My ex-woman friend has gone off to Saigon of all places, leaving me with her ghost and Diego's shadow. My publishers are telling me there is huge interest generated by my book, but I can't bring myself to tell them that what I have written has become a terrible reminder of someone else.

'What do you feel like?' a male friend asks me one day as the winter chill grips London. I've taken to kicking a football around a piece of parkland near the river. 'I'm disintegrating, mate, I'm disintegrating,' I tell him.

I'm where Diego's been before, down in the communal shit of one's own existence. The memory of his Uncle Cirilo rescuing him from the cesspit served as a reminder of his ability to survive, to pull through, but in my case it's the inability to put my book behind me that really hurts.

Just when I thought I'd finished with promoting the book, the phone begins to ring. For nearly two weeks Argentine journalists pursue me asking me what I think about Diego's latest fall from grace. Interest in my book has been fuelled by the arrest of Coppola and the suggestion that he is part of a major drug-smuggling ring. Diego silently grieves the imprisonment of his friend and confidant, somehow gets himself to believe that it's all part of a great conspiracy against him which includes my book. By now letters from his lawyers have gone out to several individuals whom I interviewed, pressurising them to retract their statements.

The prosecution against Coppola collapses after it is alleged that police had planted cocaine at his flat and conspired with a series of false witness statements. By then Maradona has himself given a statement declaring himself and his manager innocent, in a brief appearance before the investigating judge that shows the enduring nature of his popularity. Clerks and other staff of the court beg for his autograph and pose for a 'team' photograph with the past.

Such adulation in the past has fuelled Maradona's sense of himself as above good or evil, has given him an extraordinary power in his own country. So why is it that when my Argentine publishers ring me to invite me for another promotional road show I jump at the opportunity?

Well, I'm still fascinated by the guy, something in me tells me we're getting level, somewhere, somehow, subject and biographer must have it out, not on anyone's territory but his own where it all began, in a way neither he nor I chose nor could have even predicted.

So it is that on 2 April, preparing to board a British Airways flight to Buenos Aires, I can't help but ponder the significance of the date – fifteenth anniversary of my trial by fire as a foreign correspondent working in Buenos Aires for the *Financial Times*. April 2 1982 – the crowds, with national flags and anti-British slogans, pouring into the Plaza de Mayo, the terrible sense of shock and apprehension I felt at the thought that Argentines and English could soon be killing each other over distant islands.

On the eve of the invasion I had gone to see Maradona playing in a friendly against the Soviet Union. The chant had gone up around the River Plate stadium that 'He who doesn't jump is an Englishman.' Everyone had started jumping. And yet Argentina's number one player, not I, was destined for failure –

on the playing fields of Spain, the country where I was born. The Argentine media could lie about what was happening in the trenches, but there was little it could do about the football matches beamed live from Spain, short of blacking out the screens and risking a national riot. Glued to their TV boxes, millions of Argentines ignored the news that shells were falling on Port Stanley and that their troops were being forced to retreat. But they watched the national team go down 1-0 to Belgium and Maradona sent off in a game against Brazil – his blatant foul on an opposition defender, the humiliating climax to one of the worst performances of his international career.

Fifteen years on I'm not bouncing with a sense of commemorative celebration. Days before my departure, a veiled death threat to the English, addressed to me, is posted to my London office by someone claiming to be a Falklands War veteran.

When I lived in Argentina I used to get more threats than I care to mention. Some of them were hoaxes, but one had seemed potentially serious enough that the Foreign Office advised me to leave the country temporarily. So I ask a police contact for help: 'Can't MI5 check it out before I fly?' I plead. 'That might take at least two months,' is the answer.

At the Victoria station Gatwick check-in desk, a BA employee looks at me strangely. 'I'm sorry sir, but the computer is telling us you will be requiring a wheelchair,' she says. I find myself having to argue with her that there must be a mistake. 'Can't you see I am standing!' I say at one point, although a part of me has begun to suspect that Maradona's cast some kind of mad spell of on me.

When I arrive at Gatwick, they are calling for Dr Burns over the loudspeakers. This time the airline employee asks me: 'Will you be requiring a wheelchair, sir?' By now I am convinced this is Diego's idea of a sick joke.

★ ★ ★

After I touch down in Buenos Aires, Ignacio, head of media relations for Planeta, my Argentine publishers, seems close to breakdown. 'I've never experienced anything like this. No one wants to touch your book. They say they won't want to get on the wrong side of Diego. It's like a Mafia out there.'

In fact, Ezequiel Fernandes-Moores, a sports columnist with *Pagina 12*, interviews me within hours. Ezequiel has been through a few rough rides himself as the unauthorised biographer of another Argentine hero, the boxer Oscar Bonavena, who was shot dead in a Las Vegas brothel. But nothing prepares us for what happens next.

While we talk over a cup of coffee in the lobby of my hotel, I catch sight of Carlos Bilardo, the former coach of the Argentine national squad. Some English fans may remember that Bilardo's roots in the tough, no-nonsense school of Argentine football – where anything is permissible as long as it secures victory – had an early example when he played for Estudiantes, the Argentine champions of the 1960s. In a game between Estudiantes and Manchester United, Bilardo head-butted Nobby Stiles, leaving it up to his mate, Carlos Pachame, to kick open Bobby Charlton's shin.

I hold no ill-feelings towards Bilardo. While Ardiles had refused to be interviewed by me for my book (arguing 'the problem about writing a book about Maradona is that the truth hurts'), Bilardo had given me an hour of his time, providing me with some useful perspectives on Mexico 1986. It's something Maradona does not like. He has got his lawyers to write a letter to Bilardo (and indeed all the others who were interviewed by me) threatening action unless he denies ever talking to me.

I want to say hello to Bilardo, thank him in some way for helping me out, but Diego has got to him first. Nobby never had it like this.

'Hi, Carlos. Remember me, Jimmy Burns who came to

interview you about Diego?' I extend my hand in friendship.

Bilardo takes it, then pulls away when he recognises me. 'Yes, I remember you. You're a son of a bitch. Fuck out of this country.' He seems as if he's about to hit me but decides on a final line of abuse before walking away. 'We should have cut your balls off.'

The exchange is described in censored form by Fernandes-Moores in his newspaper the next morning. 'Burns has been warned that launching *Hand of God* in Argentina is not going to be an easy task,' he writes.

Day 3. I'm beginning to feel like Diego does after coming down from coke, a sense of creeping paranoia, fuelled by the surrealism of the Argentine media. Today, a journalist begins a live TV radio interview with me by quoting from a Borges poem about the Falklands War. It's about a Brit and an Argie killed in action who were more like each other than they ever realised. 'They could have been friends,' says the poem, 'but they only saw each other's faces once, on some islands that were far too famous, each one was Cain, and each one was Abel. They buried them together. Snow and ashes know them. What I have just recounted belongs to an event we cannot understand.'

I'm thinking of the relevance of all this. Am I meant to be starting another Falklands War over Diego? Are we like the characters of the poem – Juan Lopez and John Ward – interchangeable, symbiotic, biographer/subject, subject/biographer . . .

'Mr Burns are you there? Can you hear me? Are you all right,' the radio interviewer asks.

I want to say 'You've thrown me, you fucker, just like you wanted to do.' But what I say instead is 'Yes I'm here, it's just that I was really moved for a moment there.'

Then the phone-in begins. A woman in a shrill voice says: 'I think Burns has come to rob us of the one thing that belongs to us.' Another contributor says: 'You're a son of a bitch.' Then enter stage right Guillermo Coppola, Maradona's manager recently released from prison. Coppola is live and dangerous. 'Burns is a liar, and everything in the book is lies,' Coppola declares to a prime-time national radio audience.

'Have you read the book?' I ask Coppola over the airwaves. He admits he has not.

At supper that night with some old Argentine friends, conversation revolves around the power of myths in contemporary Argentina. 'People here still think the topic of whether or not Evita died a virgin is a serious political issue,' a journalist working with an Argentine TV channel says.

Day 4. Maradona collapses during a TV show in Chile. Drugs overdose? Heart attack? No, it's all OK, says Coppola, just the heat in the studio. Ignacio finds more local journalists prepared to talk to me.

Day 5. A pre-recorded interview for one of Argentina's leading football programmes. The journalist asking the questions admits that most of my answers will be heavily edited. I ask him what the problem is? 'You've written a book about politics, about drugs, about Mafias. It's a touchy subject here. We won't broadcast it because Diego might react badly,' he says.

Another phone-in. My interviewer is a former female model called Tete, who now runs a very successful afternoon chat show. My book lies on the table in front of her, crisp and unread. She looks clearly bored with the subject of football, but declares her professional duty to tackle a subject that is causing a bit of domestic bother. Once again, Coppola is called upon live to give his expert opinion. Once again Maradona's manager accuses me of lying. He is followed by Maradona's former accountant, Marcos Franchi, whom I interviewed in October 1995. He accuses me of inventing the meeting.

I go and see Luis Moreno Ocampo, a local lawyer I had befriended during the trial of the military juntas for human rights violations after the Falklands conflict. He was then deputy state prosecutor.

He tells me he is now a TV star and offers to mediate between Franchi and me by having us on his programme. 'You'll do wonders for my ratings!' he quips.

Moreno Ocampo's show is called *Forum*; guests say what they like about each other after signing a statement that bars legal action. In a country where proving libel is lengthy and costly, the offer attracts me as a way of straightening the record. Franchi admits over the phone that I had interviewed him, but backs out of the programme.

Day 6. A photographer insists on having me pose, balancing a football on my head, just like Maradona. We are in the middle of Florida, Buenos Aires' main shopping precinct. I strike a ridiculous figure, a skinny, most unsporting figure in a suit, but the hand of God ensures that I hold the ball there long enough for the motor drive to click ten frames. But I'm getting tired now of all the circus, back to thinking on Mailer, *The Prisoner of Sex*, prisoner of Diego – 'fame was your phone ringing a few times more each week to request interviews you did not wish to give . . . fame was the inhibition of taking a piss in a strange alley for fear of cops and headlines . . .'

I am driven to a piece of open ground near La Recoleta cemetery, where parts of Evita's body have been buried from time to time over the years. There, a man with a baseball cap and a large microphone leads another strike on behalf of the Maradona camp. Questioning my right to write the book, he asks: 'How would the English feel if an Argentine turned up and wrote a book about Prince Charles and Lady Di?' I think they would love it, I answer.

Day 7. My last night in Buenos Aires and halfway through it

I forget I have a last interview at breakfast time. You could say it's a typical Diego night. I'm surrounded by music, booze, women, joints, lines of coke dragged deep into the bright lights of the city from hell. A bunch of us end up in a hotel room, plundering the minibar, watching the dawn rise over the River Plate, and then it's the interview, just me and a microphone – silent and threatening – words failing me, trying to express the anger I feel towards the whole world ganging up on me, as Maradona's dad-in-law tells listeners to boycott the book.

Postscript. First day back in London. Spring is in the air but I feel wasted. An Argentine friend living in England receives a phone call from Coppola. 'Why did you give Jimmy such a rough time, Guillermo?' she asks.

'Why, all we want from him is a 30 per cent cut,' says Coppola.

And then I'm in some London bookstore clutching a copy of the paperback of my book that has just come out, feeling that a part of it belongs to someone else. I'm telling myself I've been reminded of the excitement and limitations of the game. I've loved and hated Diego. I'm coming out of the shit I was landed in by someone I loved. I'm going to tread more carefully alongside those who make football an obsession. I've thrown away the postcard from Saigon.

the battle of wounded knee

SIMON VEKSNER

John Skinner switched off the BMW's engine and sat back in his seat to collect his thoughts. Cup semi-final week. Just five days to get the players ready. Big week. The biggest week of his career.

He looked at his watch. 7.30 a.m. The car park was empty apart from the inevitable presence of Featherstone's Mercedes. The manager was at his desk at seven every morning, he was notorious for it. Skinner himself had arrived an hour earlier than usual for a Monday – he had a lot to do. Aside from Burgoyne there were several others who would need some considerable work if they were going to make it for the semi.

But Burgoyne was the key.

Without the erratic Geordie genius they were almost certain to lose the match. Featherstone would blame Burgoyne's absence for the defeat, and he'd blame Burgoyne's absence on Skinner and his team.

And as Skinner was 60, his contract up for renewal, he could expect to be parking his BMW at some Nationwide League training ground next season. If lucky.

Skinner began walking towards his office.

Last Saturday's game had been a hard-fought 1-1 draw, very tough on the players, and three first-teamers were now doubtful for the semi. And Burgoyne, well . . .

Skinner unlocked his office and, after making himself a cup of tea, he put on a video of the game, fast-forwarded to the Burgoyne incident, and watched it several times at half-speed.

Finally, Skinner let the tape run on and, as always, was amused and not a little thrilled to see himself on the screen, briefcase under his arm, bow-tie flapping, rushing on to the pitch as he had done so many times before in his 22 years as club psychotherapist.

'The Psych's having a look at him,' said the commentator. 'He's got his briefcase open and out comes the magic notepad. And Burgoyne's shaking his head. It looks bad. Yes, they're calling for the couch to be brought on. Just twenty-six minutes gone, and it looks like Saul Burgoyne will be taking no further part in this match. Trevor?'

'Well, this will be a blow for them, of course, as most of their play does seem to go through Burgoyne, doesn't it, but the real worry is whether this could put him in doubt for the semi-final, he doesn't seem to have been in my opinion *fully* sane all season—'

Skinner pressed stop.

Yes, what a season it had been for Saul Burgoyne. The lad was one of the most madness-prone players Skinner had ever worked with. Sometimes, Burgoyne's agoraphobia had been so bad that he'd needed intensive counselling right up until kick-off before he could even take the field.

And twice this season Skinner had accompanied the player to see a specialist, Dr Ufer in Vienna, for his persecution complex. Even so, Burgoyne complained regularly that opposition players were 'out to get him' and that he 'needed more protection from the referee'.

Skinner took another slurp of his tea, and his mind went back to those first few seconds, when he'd first reached the lad on the pitch.

'What are you feeling?' he'd asked.

'Me knee, me knee,' squealed the lad. 'Knee,' Skinner wrote in his pad.

'And how do you feel about your knee?' continued Skinner, initially suspecting perhaps some form of body-image distortion.

'It, it *hurts*,' Burgoyne had whispered, in a frightened voice.

Skinner finished his tea and opened his filing cabinet, which contained detailed records on the mental condition of every player and what counselling he had received during this difficult season, in which the squad had been heavily depleted by madness.

Skinner had to make a report to Featherstone at six o'clock and after an hour or so of preparation he began his usual thorough examination of all the players, questioning each in turn on the couch.

First in was Rodney Mule, the stalwart central defender. He'd missed much of the season through madness and, now in the twilight of his career, was naturally desperate to be sane for the semi-final. But a series of second-half clashes with City's fiery striker seemed to have aggravated the big defender's schizophrenia, a problem he'd been battling throughout his career. He was doubtful.

Next in was Reid, the club captain. Reidy had picked up a mild phobia but it looked as if it would respond to treatment.

The other worry was young Brown. He seemed a bit dazed, which was understandable after coming on and scoring the equaliser on Saturday. He'd suffered delusions about playing for England and marrying his girlfriend. But it was probably just a minor touch of egotism which would be fine in a couple of days.

Skinner had saved Burgoyne 'til last.

Timidly, the lad entered Skinner's consulting room which, like all Premier League consulting rooms, boasted the very latest equipment: brand-new leather couch, mahogany standard-lamp, swivel chair for the Psych and a wall-full of the finest psycho-therapeutic literature available.

'Lie down, please,' said Skinner and the lad obediently took his place on the couch. Skinner sat in his chair, facing, as ever, away from the player. 'How do you feel?' he asked.

'I can't explain it,' said Burgoyne, somewhat hesitantly.

'You can't explain it,' repeated Skinner, who was very strictly non-directive.

'No. It doesn't feel like my obsessive compulsive disorder's gone off again. Or the persecution. It's just my knee. My knee doesn't feel right. It's kind of . . . *hurting*.'

Skinner stopped taking notes. 'Your knee's hurting?'

'Suddenly, the big-hearted Geordie bursts into tears. 'Oh please,' he sobbed. 'You've got to help me, I'm so confused, I feel like I'm going injured!'

'Now, now,' said Skinner, rather alarmed at this kind of talk.

'I am! I'm injured! I'm going to need to see a doctor or have physiotherapy or something, aren't I!' shouted the midfielder, turning to look at Skinner, which he knew full well was against the rules.

But it seemed the rules no longer applied, so Skinner put a hand on the boy's shoulder. He felt every sympathy for him. To a lad of Burgoyne's working-class background, the idea of so-called 'physical injury' was shameful. Unheard-of.

'If it turns out you need a doctor, the club will find you one, the best in the country, don't you worry about that,' promised Skinner. 'Just rest for now, OK?'

'OK,' said the lad, and he hobbled off the couch. It was clear. He was injured all right – injured as a cripple.

Then came the meeting with Featherstone. A strict Scots Presbyterian, Featherstone drank only very rarely but nevertheless he offered the dapper psychotherapist a whisky on entering his office.

'So. The semi-final of the FA Cup,' said Featherstone, pouring a finger-and-a-half into the cut-glass tumbler.

'Thank you, yes,' said Skinner, wondering how long it would be before Featherstone asked about Burgoyne.

'How's Mule?' asked Featherstone.

'Well, both you and I know he'd run through a brick wall for this club. But the lad's mind's a complete wreck.'

'Could he play, with an anti-hallucinogenic injection?'

'It's a possibility. He's done it before. Played on despite severe voices. But this time he'd be risking a complete break-down and I can't allow it. It might damage his sanity irreparably in later life.'

'But that's a decision for the player, is it not?' asked Feather-stone.

Skinner paused, aware that the wily Scot had outflanked him. 'Yes, it is.' And they both knew what decision Mule would make.

'And Brown?'

'He'll be fine.'

It was clear to Skinner now that Featherstone was avoiding talking about Burgoyne until the two men had finished their whisky.

'You're a talented psychotherapist, John,' said Featherstone. 'The best in the Premiership, in my opinion.'

'Thanks, Alan.'

'I remember last year when half the squad came down with paranoia, yet somehow we managed to put out a team of eleven sane players. Then there was Reidy's grassophobia, which could have ended his career, were it not for your intervention.'

Skinner finished his whisky.

'Another?' asked Featherstone.

'Thank you,' said Skinner.

Sure enough, as soon as he'd poured the second whisky, Featherstone steered the conversation towards Burgoyne. 'What about Saul?'

'Bad, I'm afraid.' Almost unconsciously, Skinner looked over to check the door was closed.

'It's perfectly safe to talk in here,' said Featherstone.

'OK, Boss,' said Skinner. 'The fact is, I've examined him very closely. We all know he's one of the most madness-prone players in the Premiership. But this time, I can't find anything *mentally* wrong with him.'

'So what's the problem?'

'Boss, he's suffering from some kind of "physical" injury. I'm not an expert in these matters, but I would say it could be something to do with his knee. He has a "wounded" knee.'

Featherstone leaned back in his chair and began turning the tumbler in his hand, so Skinner continued: 'Despite what the press and public may believe, players *do* occasionally suffer from physical injury. After all, a footballer's body is subject to the same pressures as an ordinary man's – maybe more so. A football player doesn't just have a mind – he has a body too, and that body can suffer wear and tear.'

Featherstone put down his glass very gently on the table and cocked his head to one side.

'How long have you been in the game, John?' he asked.

'Twenty-five years.'

'Well I've been forty-one years, both as a player and a manager. You don't think I'd be totally unaware of the phenomenon of physical injury, do you?'

'No.'

'Believe me, I've come across it before. Many times. But this game is too important for the club. I can't have our best player missing because of some nebulous "knee problem". I am relying on you to get Burgoyne "fit", if that's the correct word, for this game.'

'Me? Alan, I don't think you understand. This player is *injured*. He needs a doctor, not a therapist.'

'I'm sorry, John. But you know what would happen if we

got him a doctor. The media would be all over it. I can see the headline now: "Burgoyne To See Saw-Bones." Think of the effect that would have on morale. And what about the lad himself? He'd get called a freak. It could destroy his career. You're just going to have to do what you can for him yourself.'

'I can't. I know nothing of medicine.'

'Oh come on, John. You're a healer. A healer of the mind, yes, but still a healer. Burgoyne is sick, and I want you to heal him.' Featherstone drained the rest of his whisky. 'There'll be a new contract in it for you.'

'And if I don't?'

Featherstone opened his hands outward and smiled that grim smile of his, which more closely resembled a frown.

'Are you threatening me?'

'It's no' a threat, John – it's a plea. Don't forget, this club is a lot bigger than just you, or me, or Saul Burgoyne. This club is the fans, our fans, the best fans in the whole country, and they want to see Burgoyne take the field at Villa Park on Saturday. Now you see to it that he does.'

It was with a heavy heart that Skinner went back to check on Burgoyne, who was now in extreme denial.

'I'm not injured, me,' chirped the Geordie. 'I'm just mad, aren't I?'

Skinner smiled. 'Go home, Saul,' he said. 'Go home and see your wife. We'll talk again in the morning.'

Burgoyne was married to Samantha Busty, the former page three model.

Skinner sighed. It had been a long day and it was time for him to go home and talk things over with his own wife.

'Hello, Sparrow,' said Skinner, putting his arms around his wife.

'Hard day, Chicken?' she asked.

Skinner explained about Burgoyne's knee, the offer of a new contract, and the rest. His wife remained silent for a time, solemnly stirring the casserole.

'What does this new contract mean to you?' she asked finally.

'Everything,' said Skinner. 'It looks like I've missed my chance for the England job now. At least if I get this contract I'll be able to retire in three years, we can pay off the mortgage, and have enough left over for that trip round the world we've always promised ourselves. If I don't, it'll mean dropping down a division. Maybe two. The salary will be lower and I'll have to keep on working for another five or six years.'

'And what does this game mean to the club?'

'Everything. We haven't been in the Cup final for twenty years, let alone won it.'

Skinner trusted his wife's judgement implicitly. Though she cared nothing for football and never followed it on the radio or TV, she was extremely good at sorting through moral dilemmas.

'On the one hand,' explained Skinner, 'I want what's best for the team. That means Burgoyne playing. But I also want what's best for the player and he shouldn't play unless he sees a doctor and Featherstone won't let him see one.'

'Can you do for him what a doctor could do for him?'

'I don't think so. I know very little about the "black arts" of physiotherapy.'

'Could you find out?'

'I could try. Yes, that's what I'll do. I'll go to the library. Do some reading.'

'Starling, you do whatever you think's best.'

Once in the library, Skinner headed furtively for the medical textbooks section.

He found a couple of books that seemed suitable, flicked through them, daunted by the strange terms such as 'Achilles Tendon' and 'Ankle Ligament', and headed for the club.

In the afternoon he saw Burgoyne. First, he looked closely at the lad's knee. Then he referred to his notes. Could it be a cruciate problem? What were the symptoms of that? He looked down at Burgoyne, who was grinning up at him with idiotic faith. Skinner did his best to smile back but he felt lost. After getting the lad to 'flex' his knee, Skinner 'palped' the muscles, a procedure which made both men feel uncomfortable and which illuminated nothing for the psychotherapist.

In the end, Skinner gave up and spent half an hour asking Burgoyne questions about his childhood and uncovering a few minor latent traumas, which cheered them both up immensely. At least the player would be fully sane by Saturday, even if he was injured.

At the end of the day, Skinner felt drained and he was glad finally to get back to his car, but he found someone there waiting for him. It was Terry Terrett, chief football reporter of the *Daily Raker*.

'Can we talk?' asked the hack, in his gruff Cockney manner.

'Of course,' said Skinner.

Skinner shut the car door and turned to face him.

'I know the truth about Burgoyne,' said Terrett. 'He's not insane at all. He's got some kind of knee injury or something.'

There were rumours that Terrett was having an affair with Samantha Busty – it was no doubt by that route he had found out the truth.

'I can't comment,' said Skinner. 'But you seem pretty sure of your facts; I wonder why you need me to say anything.'

Terrett coughed. 'I need official confirmation from the club's psychotherapist.'

'Why? Because Samantha Busty would kill you if the story came out?'

Terrett pulled out a packet of cigarettes and fumbled to strike a match. 'You've guessed it,' he admitted.

'I'm a psychotherapist, Terry. It's my job to know the minds of men. Do you love her?'

'I do. The last thing I want is to hurt her. But I also need this story. "Burgoyne In Physiotherapy" would be the football scoop of the year.'

'I'm afraid I can't help you. Sorry.'

'I understand,' said Terrett.

And with that, Skinner got into his car.

Driving home, he was deep in thought – Burgoyne, the club, Miss Busty, Terrett, Featherstone . . .

'Oi! Baldy! You with the glasses and the funny beard!'

He looked over – there were six or seven youths yelling from the pavement, drunk, a couple of them wearing United shirts.

'Uni-*ted*, Uni-*ted*,' they started singing. 'We're on our way to Wem-bley . . .'

They must have recognised him from the TV – one of them threw a half-full can of lager in his direction.

Quickly, he accelerated away.

Once home he made himself some tea, sat in his armchair and tried to relax, but he kept imagining what Samantha Busty would have said to Terrett. In his head he heard her uncultured tones, grating through the monstrously tacky decor of the home she shared with Burgoyne on the Essex/Hertfordshire border: 'My Saul, 'e's fragile. I don't want the 'ole country knowin' 'e's got, I carn't even say it, *physical* problems.'

Skinner was still pondering the situation when he heard his wife's key turn in the lock as she returned from her evening class.

'Good evening, Chaffinch,' said his wife, planting a kiss on his cheek.

Skinner smiled weakly.

'Oh dear,' said his wife. 'Problems?'

'I'm afraid so, my little Swallow,' said Skinner, and briefly updated her on all that had happened. 'So it seems,' concluded Skinner, 'that I have a moral obligation to obtain medical treatment for the player.'

'I would say so,' agreed his wife. Skinner began scratching the back of his hand. 'But that's not the only thing on your mind, is it, my Ostrich?'

'No, you're right,' said Skinner. 'I shall make an anonymous tip-off to the press. This taboo about physical ill-health – it's ridiculous, and it must be brought to an end. Burgoyne's injury is the perfect opportunity to bring the matter to the attention of the media, and thereby the general public.'

'Quite right,' agreed his wife. 'And I'm so proud that it will be you, Hummingbird of my life, who will go on the record to do so.'

'On the record?' queried Skinner.

'Of course,' snorted Mrs Skinner. 'Otherwise Samantha Busty will assume the story came from Terrett and no doubt end their relationship.'

'But what about my new contract – and our dream holiday?'

His wife came over to join him, eased her considerable frame on to his spindly knee and tugged gently at his beard.

'This is more important. And that's what I love about you, my Robin. You always put principles first. In the end.'

The very next day, Skinner smuggled Burgoyne out of the club and booked him into an exclusive clinic where Britain's top pop stars and actors were treated for sprained ankles, broken ribs and the like. The doctors assured him that, with proper physiotherapy, Burgoyne might even be able to play on Saturday.

Of course, Skinner said nothing of all this to Alan Feather-stone, merely reporting that the player was making good progress. But on the eve of the semi-final, Skinner duly called Terrett at the *Raker*.

'I believe "Hold The Back Page" is the appropriate phrase,' said Skinner.

They met in a car park on the outskirts of Birmingham.

'I'm prepared to go on the record and say that Burgoyne is quite sane and that his problems are purely physical,' said Skinner. 'I will tell you everything.'

'You do realise that Featherstone will be mad at you?' asked Terrett, who reached into his pocket, brought out his Dicta-phone and, all in one smooth movement, switched it on.

'I do,' said Skinner. 'But this issue needs bringing to the public's attention.'

After the interview was finished, Terrett had one question for Skinner.

'Look, I can't thank you enough, John. You've given me the best story of my career. And you've saved my bacon with Miss Busty. Now – is there anything I can do for you?'

'No,' said Skinner firmly. 'As I said, it's enough for me that the issue is brought to public attention.'

That night, Skinner returned to the team's hotel and had the most peaceful night's sleep he had had for some time. He was rudely awoken at 7.05 a.m.

'Downstairs – now.' It was Featherstone. He must have seen the papers already.

Skinner made his way to the conference room that the Scot was using as a temporary office. Featherstone motioned for Skinner to sit down, though he himself remained standing. It was headmaster's study time.

'Behind my back,' began Featherstone without preamble,

'you send Burgoyne to some Saw-Bones. And as if that were no' bad enough, you blab to the press. Now, please tell me, because I have to say I'm curious, why did you do it?'

'Look, Alan, I know you don't think so right now, but I've done the right thing. Yes, the press story will be a shock to the lads but the important thing is that Burgoyne is fit to play and his long-term health has not been jeopardised.'

'But *physical injury*?' spat Featherstone. 'What do you want to open that can of worms for?'

'Maybe it'll start to become accepted as normal. Maybe it won't be such a can of worms in the future.'

'Well,' said Featherstone. 'It's a future that you'll be observing from the lower divisions.'

'I realise that,' said Skinner, looking the manager straight in the eye.

'You won't be on the bench today. You can go home if you like,' said Featherstone.

'I'll watch from the stand,' said Skinner, and he went back up to his hotel room.

Skinner took a long, leisurely bath and then decided to trim his beard, and after the 8.30 news who should he hear but Alan Featherstone being interviewed on BBC Radio Five Live: 'Now, I want to talk about the sanity situation at the club, if you don't mind, Alan,' said the interviewer.

'Certainly. Rodney Mule has only a fifty/fifty chance of being sane for the game. He's got a psychotic personality which is badly in need of rest, and if he plays it'll be with an anti-hallucinogenic injection. Brown picked up a knock in training, a slight blow to his self-esteem which has been giving him a little bit of unconfidence, but he should shake it off. Reidy faces a late sanity test, but we expect him to come through. He's been battling for sanity all season, but I would say he's virtually back to full sanity now and will be sane to play today.'

'And what about the situation everyone's talking about – Burgoyne? There are stories in the paper today about Saul Burgoyne possibly suffering from a "physical injury"?'

'Yes, well, a lot's been made of that in certain sections of the media—'

'But it was your own club psychotherapist, John Skinner, who made those remarks—'

'Yes, and John's a good professional, who's been with the club many years now, but all I'll say is that you will see Burgoyne out on the pitch this afternoon.'

'And he'll get you to the final?'

'He'll get us to the final, yes.'

'Alan Featherstone, thank you very much.'

'Thank you.'

Skinner laughed and turned the radio off. Then the phone rang. It was his wife.

'Have a look in *The Authoritarian*,' she said.

'*The Authoritarian*?'

'*The Authoritarian*. That's all I'm saying.'

She hung up. Skinner left his hotel room. He ran into a few of the players but none of them had seen *The Authoritarian* – they didn't take much interest in the broadsheets – so Skinner picked up a copy in the hotel shop and, turning to the sports section of *The Authoritarian*, sister paper to *The Raker*, he found a long article by Terry Terrett, praising Skinner for bringing the issue of players' physical health out into the open. He even tipped Skinner as the next England psychotherapist!

He thought back to the brief conversation he'd just had with his wife. What on earth, he wondered, had she been doing reading the sports section?

my life after eric

JIM WHITE

There is a scene in Andy Hamilton's sublime comedy film *Eleven Men Against Eleven* which catches a traditionalist old coach, played by James Bolam, as he sits watching television. Bolam's character is an old-fashioned football man marooned by the tidal wave modernisation of the game swishing around him and, as he sits, he lists his complaints about the game today: 'Middle-class wankers writing novels about the emotional aspects of supporting Arsenal, endless imaginary leagues of pretend teams, full-backs with number 38 on their shirts.' But the evidence that finally confirms for him that football has lost all contact with planet earth arrives when, as he watches, a television presenter asks Patsy Kensit her opinion of the flat back four.

'Christ,' he says, the fight visibly seeping from him. 'Now I've seen everything.'

Well, I've got news for James Bolam's dispirited Luddite: I've seen worse. I've seen Mad Frankie Fraser being asked by a television interviewer for his reaction to the retirement of Eric Cantona.

It happened at the launch party of the book *The Meaning of Cantona* by Terence Blacker and Willie Donaldson. This was an occasion with all the requirements of a decent literary promotion: there was plentiful wine, a handy supply of mini taramasalata pastries and His Madness himself. The Richardsons' enforcer, once reckoned the most violent man in Britain, the geezer who made a speciality of removing rivals' teeth with a pair of gold-plated pliers purchased at Harrods; since he had his autobiography published, Frankie Fraser is often seen at bookish functions. He chats amiably with softie writers who feel their day has been made conversing with a real-life murderer. I know because I'm one of them.

'Let me give you a word of advice, author to author,' he said to me. And when Frankie speaks, you tend to listen. 'Every time you pass a book store, go in and ask the manager if you can sign copies of your book. Because when they're signed, they cannot be remaindered.'

He had something, incidentally. A couple of months later, I happened to be in a book shop in Islington, and there on the counter was a tottering Canary Wharf of unsold volumes of *Mad Frankie*. On top was a note which read 'signed copies'.

The party was held two days after Eric Cantona had announced his retirement from football: good timing, the publisher reckoned, lots of publicity would accrue. And there were a couple of television crews spinning in among the revellers, filming them chatting animatedly about Eric and his meaning. The reporter from Sky Television was anxious to put a fundamental question to guests: never mind the footballing establishment, would the literary world recover from the unexpected departure of Cantona from the scene? And the man he first sought to quiz was the murderous gangster in our midst.

'Well, it'll be hard without him, I'm not saying it won't be,' Frankie expounded. 'He was an inspirational figure for us writers and what you might call intellectuals. No doubt about it, he will be missed.'

And the bizarre thing is, he was right.

Over the past five years, as he has strode through our lives, chest out, head up, shoulders back, a cottage industry has grown up around Eric Cantona. On my shelves at home, there are eight books about him. I alone must have written about 50,000 words on the player (not different ones, the word 'genius' tends to get repeated a lot). On the day he announced his retirement, I was asked by four newspapers and magazines and five radio and television programmes for my views. A producer from Radio 4's Sunday morning media show 'Mediumwave' rang to ask me to do a piece about it.

'I'm not quite sure what there is to say,' she said. 'But I kind of feel we must say something.'

Kerching: another £100. There's no doubt about it, Eric's been good for me. And not just me, but others have used him to appease their bank managers. Writers like Ian Ridley (author of *Cantona: The Red And The Black*) and Richard Kurt (author of the more directly titled *Cantona*), not to mention Michael Browne, the Manchester artist whose 12-foot high oil painting of Cantona as the risen Christ was bought by the man himself for £80,000. Or Peter Boyle, the cheer-leader of Old Trafford's K-Stand, who recorded two albums of tune-free songs about Eric. And named his child after him. What are we all going to do without him?

When I left the *Independent* newspaper, as is the tradition, the lads there mocked up a front page as a leaving card. It was fantastic. Eric's Selhurst Park kung fu assault was reproduced to fill the entire page. But where Matthew Simmons's leery mug should have been, a photo of my face, grinning inanely, had been superimposed. The headline read: 'Cantona attacks stalker.'

Funny, but not quite right. True enough, for these past five years I've been following him, watching, observing, taking in his every move. But a stalker seeks to intrude on his target's life; I've been more like a Peeping Tom. Or as Eric would put it: I was the seagull following the trawler.

My entire relationship with Eric Cantona runs as follows. On the plane shared by the players and press to Istanbul for

Manchester United's ill-starred game against Galatasaray in November 1994, I found myself returning from the lavatory to be confronted by Eric coming down the aisle towards me. It says in all the statistics books that he's six foot two. But he seemed much bigger there on the plane, huge he was, filling up the space.

'Pardon,' I said, in creaking schoolboy French as we came nose to chin.

'Ça va,' he said, shrugging past me, non-committally.

And the second time was a year later, in the Nou Camp after United's embarrassing trashing by Barca. In a perfect example of reputation being advanced by absence, Eric hadn't played in that game, thanks to a ban for his sending-off in Turkey. Thus he couldn't be held responsible for the rout. In the vast media room in the bowels of the stadium, a space crammed with reporters circling Ronald Koeman, Romario and Jordi Cruyff, the glowing victors, I spotted Cantona in a corner talking with another French observer. He was in earnest conversation (you assume he can't have any other kind). Sensing an exclusive – all the other English correspondents were filing their copy – I approached the pair.

'Sorry, Eric, I erm was just wondering if . . .' I said.

By the way of response he stuck out his bottom lip, shook his head and made a brisk shooing movement with his hand. This was long before Selhurst, before the assault on Brent Sadler, two years before he took out that French photographer in Cannes. But he didn't need a reputation to make it plain he didn't want to talk.

That was it, that was the sum total of our direct relationship. Yet on the day he announced he was off, out of Old Trafford without so much as a farewell, I felt bereft: sorry for myself facing up to life without him. Who's interesting now?

★ ★ ★

Even if you were Max Clifford you could not have arrived at an image-generating methodology quite as successful as Eric's. It was not simply that everything he did merited discussion. You have read the biographies, you know the story: the poetry, the painting, the philosophy; the trail of sulphur, the flung boots, the leap into the crowd; the sublime moments of skill mixed with the savagery. It was more that he instinctively knew how the modern media worked, knew how to keep himself the centre of attention.

Eric's fame was principally established by saying nothing. The British media, with its proliferation of outlets, of chat shows and phone-ins, magazine exclusives and book serialisations, offers an unending, uncritical employment opportunity for the loudmouth. How else do you explain the career of Dominik Diamond? For a man with an ego bloated to the size of a diseased bladder, Cantona might have seemed a natural for the spout circuit. In the brilliant film *When We Were Kings* you can see how Muhammad Ali bolstered his sense of self through contact with the media: he held press conferences for hours in front of an adoring entourage hanging on his every gag, with otherwise robust writers like Hugh McIlvanney hoping the next line of poetry would centre on them. Indeed the film finishes with Norman Mailer retelling an anecdote about a brief encounter with Ali which clearly qualifies as one of the outstanding memories of the author's wonderful career.

Cantona felt no such need to be reckoned a hero by the media. He treated us in the press corps almost universally with contempt. Perhaps this isn't surprising given some of the vituperative coverage he endured in his time, and given that he was guided by a team manager whose paranoia with the press verges on the clinical. But it certainly wasn't because he was a recluse. I know of dozens of incidental moments of kindness he showed to fans: going out of his way to sign autographs, taking time out to visit those in hospital, never losing patience when he ran into lads out on the town in Manchester who wanted to prostrate themselves at his feet.

Approach him as a journalist, though, and the response was non-existent. Believe me, I tried. I wrote to him on a dozen occasions requesting interviews for every publication from *Esquire* to the *Independent Magazine*. I was never even granted the courtesy of a reply. Yet I know of fans who had a hand-addressed response to their mail within a week. It wasn't just me. At the Football Writers' Dinner, the yearly beer-up where the leading hacks assemble and assume themselves at the centre of footballing things, it is standard for the winner of the Foot-baller of the Year award to hang around afterwards, to chat to his tormentors in the press, sign autographs, make himself available. In 1995, I saw Jürgen Klinsmann – generally assumed the master of public relations – stand there for hours humouring a long line of sycophants who queued up for signatures ('It's not for me, Jürgen, you understand, it's for my daughter. Yes, she's called John too'). By contrast, in 1996 Cantona uttered a short speech ('when there is criticism, I roll it up and throw it down the toilet') then turned on his heels, the award under his arm, and left, pausing only to sign a menu for a waiter.

Yet his very silence and brusqueness intrigued us all. Like nature, the media abhors a vacuum, and into the space vacated by any word from him poured a hundred theories. The amateur psychologist in us all had not so much a field day as a fortnight, all expenses paid, in Ibiza. No one writing this stuff knew what he was really like, none of us had talked to him long enough to establish a plausible theory, but the speculation was presented as cast-iron fact.

These are a few of the readings of the player offered up during his career in England.

1. I still think Cantona will let you down at the highest level.

He's a cry-baby when the going gets tough. (George Graham, 1994)

2. The talk among your fellow professionals is that you are steadily becoming a nasty, dirty bastard. (John Fashanu, 1994)

3. I'd have his balls cut off. (Brian Clough, 1995)

4. Eric is no longer a footballer, he is an issue. He is either loved or hated like a chart-topping teeny-band. (Jimmy Greaves, 1995)

And my favourite:

5. Given Cantona's intellectuality, perhaps the surest way to wind him up would be to challenge him on a philosophical basis. It may well turn out that what Matthew Simmons actually shouted was: 'Eric! Your concept of individuality is grossly diluted! You fail to acknowledge the despair pendant upon the absurdity of the human predicament! Abandon your semi-consciousness! You're acquiescent and you know you are! Come and have a go if you think you're Sartrian enough!' (Giles Smith, *Independent on Sunday*, 1995)

In his humorous thrust, Giles Smith makes the most telling point. For the self-appointed clever-clogs increasingly drawn to the game, Eric was a godsend of a footballer. Because he did not share the vernacular of the workplace, knew nothing about being gutted or about how appearing in a Cup final is obviously what you dream about as a professional footballer all your career; because he indulged in none of the wearisome false modesty of the English player ('well I just kinda stuck me foot out and it flew in, they never do in training'); because he made occasional allusions that were unexpected ('the touch of the ball is like the caress of a woman'); because he read a book rather than played cards on the team bus; and most of all because he was French, he was taken to be an intellectual. The French themselves, incidentally, perhaps because he was less reticent in his mother tongue, were not so impressed. Hidden shallows, they reckoned.

'I'm not sure about his cultural knowledge,' Claude Simonet, president of the French Football Association said in 1994. 'It seems pretty basic to me.' Fair enough, M Simonet. A bit of Rimbaud, a pinch of Mickey Rourke, seasoned with some Maradona and James Dean is the standard misunderstood youth stuff. But for the English observer it made a hell of a change from *Grange Hill*, *FHM* and Labatt's Ice, those standard cultural influences on the British player.

The apogee of this fascination is the book Frankie Fraser was celebrating when he was collared by the television cameras. *The Meaning of Cantona* is a wry and cunning volume listing hundreds of Eric aphorisms ('Cantona does not wear his collar turned up; everyone else wears theirs turned down'). As it transpires, the phrases and sayings are not actually Cantona's own. They come from the imagination of the two authors, filling in the gaps, providing the kind of memorable epithets Eric might have uttered had they been around to record them. But since they had never met him, the pair couldn't be absolutely sure whether he had. So they made up the book, just in case he hadn't. And as they were doing so they reckoned they were providing a satirical commentary on the obsession of the modern world with cultural icons who are essentially empty. Nice one: it's called having it both ways.

None of this could have happened if Cantona had talked to Motty, Des, Dr Anthony Clare and all. Whatever prompted his initial decision to ration his public utterances – my own opinion is it was because he felt unsure of his spoken English and, being Cantona, hated the thought of being revealed publicly as having any weakness – it soon became clear this was an economic triumph. Through silence, his words achieved rarity value. Nike were the first company to appreciate this. They tellingly positioned themselves as the brand of the maverick. The message was: wear our trainers and you too could be as big a rebel as Eric Cantona. In a reversal of the standard sporting endorsement by a role model, this was affirmation by anti-hero. Probably the best of their ads, played out in moody black and white, a blues track twanging in the background, ran like this:

'I have been punished for striking a goalkeeper. For spitting at supporters. For throwing my shirt at a referee. For calling my manager a bag of shit. I called those who judged me a bunch of idiots. I thought I might have trouble finding a sponsor.'

Cantona is said to have loved those ads. No wonder: they absolutely tallied with his own self-image. For a long time I thought his every public utterance was provided by the ad agency, thus making him the first ever sportsman to be entirely scripted by an advertising copywriter. But I recently met Maurice Watkins, the Manchester United director and legal adviser who was with him on the day, who told me that Eric's most famous aphorism was arrived at on the spot, as the two of them waited to enter the press conference in Croydon Crown Court after he had successfully appealed against a jail sentence for assaulting Simmons. Eric turned to Watkins and asked him to translate a French proverb he knew, something about fishing boats and sprats. It was Watkins's rather loose interpretation which gave the phrase its surreal spin in English. But even then, I thought the seagulls and trawler represented a straightforward metaphor: Cantona was the big, significant body, we in the press were the parasites, feeding off his throwaways. Typically, though, the media excavated for profundity, to the extent of missing what I thought was the most significant moment of the whole event. In the middle of delivering his speech, Cantona paused for a sip from a glass of water. Look carefully and you could see what he was doing:

composing himself lest he corpsed in laughter. This was all a game.

Never mind the image, what most of us who treated Cantona seriously were really responding to was his prowess on the field. I believe he was responsible for the best football I have ever seen.

More than that. With nine, Phil Neal has the record for the largest collection of championship medals of any player in England. His, though, were won over a lengthy career. With five gongs in six years popped on to the sideboard (and he knows he was only denied a clean sweep by his own madness at Selhurst) Cantona's qualifies as the most significant intervention in the history of British domestic football. How George Best must look on in envy: Cantona arrived at Old Trafford at the same age Best was when he walked out.

To be accurate, the personal annexation of the statistics began at Leeds United – though these days, at Elland Road, his contribution to the club's 1992 championship has been retrospectively minimised. This is sour grapes taken to a Stalinistic level. Put simply, he scored and made important goals which accrued crucial points in the final title charge. Also, less quantifiably, though more vitally, his certainty in the dressing room ('Why should I, the great Cantona, be afraid of this competition?') steadied the nerves of his colleagues while those over the Pennines were shredding.

Since his arrival at Old Trafford in November 1992, red followers have been more inclined to offer credit where it is due. As the *Sun* would have it: it was Eric wot won it. A title and a double were achieved in 1993 and 1994 respectively under his direction. The goals, the control, the vision of the passing in those years reached a consistent level of excellence.

The standard response from non-believers to his dominant

form in the Premiership was the George Graham line: big fish, little pond, hides when the going gets harder. Though three goals in Cup finals might be sufficient on its own to undermine this argument, his form in European competition presents a problem. His were skills which might have been tailored to dominate the Premiership. In the mad hurly and hack of the English league, he took time to analyse, his speed of thought sufficient to escape the attentions of the wild lunges which constitute tackles over here. In the better reaches of Europe (Italy, Germany, Spain), where though the pace is slower, the speed of tackle is sharper, his approach was less successful. He got caught out.

Nevertheless, given that he only twice played at his peak for United in Europe (against Kispest Honved and Fenerbahce), he deserved to have twenty times more books written about him than he has had for one reason alone: his contribution to United's 1995–96 double. There were two widespread assumptions made about Cantona's return to combat in October 1995 after his nine-month Selhurst suspension. He would, sooner or later, snap again and this time would be the last. Or, if he suppressed his furies, he would discover he could not play to his old level without them; a reprise of the passion-and-fire argument once used by the man himself to excuse his excesses. Gloriously, both theories were proved wrong. Those who know Cantona say he always claimed he could control that impulse of his to correct perceived wrongs with immediate dispatch. He was wont to come back after a suspension for yet another misdemeanour and say to friends: 'This time it will be different, I've worked out a way to control myself.' Generally, his resolve lasted until he was presented with a poor referee, a stud-happy opponent, or a gobshite fan. But this time – his last chance, maybe – he stuck at it.

And more than that, he found he was a better player without the red rag flapping in front of his eyes. Arriving back at the core of a team which had been stripped of Kanchelskis, Ince and Hughes, he cajoled, inspired and at times carried his young colleagues through the season. In the run-in to the title, he scored the winner or the equaliser in 13 games, a prodigious achievement. I saw him do it against West Ham, QPR, Coventry, Spurs and, wonderfully, against Liverpool in the Cup final. Every time, it was a goal whose drama and timing forced you to leap from the seat in appreciation (not a sensible thing to do in the home section of Upton Park). But the one that really summed it up was at St James' Park, in March 1996 against a vital and effective Newcastle side. For an hour, thanks in the main to Schmeichel, United absorbed everything their rivals hurled at them. At one point, after another miracle save, Les Ferdinand (whoever he plays for, always a handful against United) sank to his knees and realised his best was just not good enough. It was a rerun of Muhammad Ali's rope-a-dope trick against George Foreman: take everything they have and appear undamaged, as if to sneer, 'Is that all you can do?' And then, to rub it in, Cantona scored, drifting into space and finishing it with the chin-seeking right hook. It wasn't just a goal that won a game, it was a goal that assassinated his rivals' hopes. And with that won a title.

Best of all, never once, through that glorious chase, or the following year, did the old Cantona temper resurface. He started to cast himself as the peace-maker on the pitch, the wise old head who would lead perplexed colleagues away from the scrap. Just as Tony Adams fights when he goes past a bar, or Paul Merson tightens his resolve when he sees a mirror on a coffee table, so Cantona must have battled to control his urges in those seasons. But he did it privately, apparently changing his character alone, through his own strength of will. That was his achievement, and it was not sufficiently acknowledged in the obituaries to his career.

★ ★ ★

In the end, nothing summed up Cantona more than the manner of his retirement. At matches towards the end of the 1997 season I saw him look puzzled on the field, perplexed, frightened even, when the flicks and feints didn't work. An intense student of his own game, Cantona realised this was not temporary lack of form, but the first indications of the inevitable abasement of the physique. He had begun to sense his own decline. And he didn't want to hang around and watch himself drift down, abdicating to the bench while Juninho or Boksic or Zidane strutted across his pitch. He wasn't one for a below-the-title credit. So out he went, at the top.

And then he underscored it all with a joke: he didn't even turn up to his own press conference to announce the decision. There was to be no heart-searching exclusive in the *Sunday Times*, no anguished revelations on Richard and Judy's sofa, just silence, walk away and leave others to explain. Then the enjoyment of the thought that even as he sat on his holiday balcony, the newspaper pages were being readied in his honour.

Which leads us back to Mad Frankie and his analysis. Now Eric's gone, who am I going to write about now? Who is there who could stage-manage events like that? Scholesy? Tidy little player, but you can't see him inspiring eight books in the next four seasons. Not unless he is hiding his light under a very large bushel.

the way they play in el dorado

JAMES WILSON

Few people have more cause to remember Faustino Asprilla's Newcastle United debut than Steve Vickers, the Middlesbrough defender. The Colombian signed for Newcastle in February 1996, after protracted negotiations, and finally arrived from Italy only a few hours before the Middlesbrough game. He had a glass of white wine and was named as a substitute, then with 23 minutes left, and Newcastle 1-0 down, he was sent into the match. He crossed himself, jogged on, and bent down to touch the Riverside Stadium turf. Then he picked the ball up on the left touchline and turned Vickers inside out before crossing to set up the Newcastle equaliser. Newcastle won the match 2-1. I imagined Steve Vickers going home that night, still shaking his head, and people saying: 'Never mind, son. Could happen to anyone.'

It is one of my fondest memories of Asprilla. The other is from a time when I was living in Colombia, in September 1993, when, in a scruffy bar run by a down-at-heel Italian, I watched Colombia play Argentina in a qualifying match for the 1994 World Cup. Argentinian fans had stoned the Colombian team bus, hurled racist insults – several Colombian players were black – and shouted all night outside their hotel. 'We loved it,' said one of the Colombians. 'We're used to noise. It was just like home.' Colombia needed a draw to qualify. They won 5-0. By the end Diego Maradona, watching from the stand, was leading the Argentinian applause.

Asprilla's second goal of the match was a work of genius. He robbed Borelli on the half-way line and had a clear run down the inside-left channel. Sergi Goycochea came a little way off his goal-line but before he could do anything Asprilla lofted the ball over him and in at the far post. He did it from 25 yards, with the outside of his right foot, without checking his stride and without even seeming to lift his foot. When I see it replayed, and when I see Asprilla running in towards the goal, I feel the hairs on the back of my neck rising. It is the best goal I have ever seen.

I suspect Kevin Keegan has also seen that goal. Certainly he was not deterred from signing Asprilla by the more lurid tales associated with him. Colombians call these *crónicas rojas*, red tales. There have been some good ones, notably:

The Porn Star. Asprilla got mixed up with a German 'actress', Petra Scharbach, during his time playing in Italy. 'Now He's Doing Handsprings in Bed!' was the headline in one Colombian newspaper at the time, referring to Asprilla's gymnastic on-field celebrations when he scores.

The Bus Incident. Asprilla went to Colombia in 1993 to see his ill mother and returned to Italy with a badly gashed foot, which he said he had cut on some glass at a swimming pool. In fact he put it through a bus window after an argument with the driver.

The Gun Owner. Asprilla was prosecuted for illegal gun possession while on another visit home and had to report to the Colombian authorities each month.

Because of these incidents Asprilla is often described as 'controversial'; because he has largely given up talking to the press after its extensive coverage of these incidents, he is also 'enigmatic'. Both these adjectives are useful substitutes for 'Colombian'. Not much is known about Colombia and I would guess it is probably the most mis-spelled country in the world, people being more familiar with the movie studio. It is a very beautiful country with a number of problems, which makes it like most countries in the world, except that Colombia is widely associated with cocaine, which gives it and its people a certain notoriety.

I returned to Colombia earlier this year, for the first time since Asprilla came to Newcastle, a few days before Colombia were due to play Paraguay in another World Cup qualifying game. I was on the bus to Asprilla's home town of Tuluá, travelling along the Panamerican Highway through a beautiful landscape of sugar canes and distant mountains, when we passed a young lad on a bicycle wearing a Newcastle shirt. There was a number 11 – Asprilla's number – on the back. In Tuluá I unpacked my own Newcastle shirt, and the hotel porter offered to buy it from me. I declined. 'Asprilla's father has one,' he said. 'He wears it when he goes to the Tuluá games.'

Asprilla was born in Tuluá in 1969. I had been led to expect a small, poverty-stricken village, but a sign boasted 155,000 inhabitants and there were no pigs rooting around the streets. Asprilla and his career are the biggest news in Tuluá; when he used to visit the whole place would go mad, with parties in which Asprilla played a prominent part. 'I used to have to ask him to warn me when he was coming back, because it caused such chaos,' I was told by writer and politician Gustavo Alvarez Guardeazábal, Tuluá's former mayor, who described himself as Asprilla's 'public defender'. It was in Tuluá that Asprilla was taunted by a bus driver, climbed out through the sunroof of his car, and put his foot through one of the bus windows. 'I told people not to be unfair with him,' Guardeazábal said. 'They had to understand that just because he was a genius at football, it didn't mean he could handle everything else. You've got to understand who he is.' Asprilla helped Guardeazábal get re-elected.

Asprilla had played for several local teams before he was bought – for about £50 and two used footballs – by the Carlos Sarmiento soccer school, which was set up with a gift from a Tuluá sugar baron. The two goalkeepers in the Colombian squad, Farid Mondragón and Miguel Calero, also went to the school. So did Oscar Córdoba, who kept goal in the 1994 World Cup. 'Tell everyone in Newcastle about the school,' said its director in nearby Cali. 'We're on the Internet.'

At one of the school's trials in Cali I watched a practice match involving about 35 kids on a bone-hard pitch. Fabio Mosquera, one of Asprilla's early coaches, was refereeing. 'He was nutty, that one,' said Mosquera. 'Head in the clouds. But at heart –' and he clapped his fist to his breast, 'he was a good kid.' Another coach, Raul, said: 'Compared to what he was, now he's a real team player.'

In Tuluá I met Fernando Valderrama. Fernando was a newly qualified trainer at the Sarmiento school when he had the young Asprilla in his group. 'He used to hate the physical stuff,' he recalled. 'I'd say, "Faustino, what's up?" and he'd say, "Aw, coach, I don't like all this running about . . ." He always wanted to be doing stuff with the ball.'

Fernando took me to the Asprilla family house. In a poorer part of the town, it is one of the few on the street with two storeys, and is big by Colombian standards. We were ushered by a maid into the cool, colourful entrance hall. On one wall was a large oil portrait of Asprilla's mother, who died just before the 1993 European Cup-Winners' Cup final. Another portrait showed Asprilla in jacket and tie, while a third pictured him in action for Parma. Light streamed from upstairs, and fell across the stairs and the turquoise painted banisters. There were stained glass windows. At the back of the house I saw a swimming pool.

'The house has been totally rebuilt,' said Fernando. Asprilla's younger sister was in – I think she said her name was Betty – but she wasn't talking to journalists. Her face wore the same look of sullen non-cooperation which appears so often on her brother's.

Asprilla's own enormous new house – built on the proceeds from the pizza restaurants and the sports shop he owns in Cali, not to mention his salary – is outside town, along an unmetalled road with the way barred by a security guard who took the taxi driver's number. Further up the road is the San Carlos sugar mill, where the Sarmiento family, who endowed the soccer school, made their money. Asprilla has called his house the Criadero Santino, the Santino Ranch – a cute amalgamation of his and his son Santiago's names (I guess Faustiago would sound a bit too dark). It is an exercise in footballer's taste – part brick, part golden stone, part wooden boards like a Dallas ranch. It has windows of tiny panes in a European style set in green painted frames. In the carport stood a Mercedes, a four-wheel-drive thing, and a sleek black sports model. Staff were tending the horses in the stable blocks. 'He has about 20 horses,' Raul had told me. Asprilla's first horse was called Ben Gurion, after the Israeli leader. In front of the house was the space reserved for the football pitch yet to be built.

I went back into Tuluá, where on the bumpy Sarmiento pitch on the edge of town, covered with thick, tropical grass, Fernando was putting about 40 kids through their paces. A lot were black and very skinny. A lot were very talented. 'All the best players are from this part of Colombia,' said Fernando. 'The ones that can do the clever things. There are some here as good as Asprilla.' Around 4,500 boys try out for the Sarmiento school each year. It takes ten or twelve, who, after a morning at regular school, travel for up to four hours each day to get to training. A house the size of Asprilla's is a powerful incentive.

Asprilla left the Carlos Sarmiento school and began his professional career in Cúcuta, a less than illustrious club who played their home games in a town 60 miles away because no one went to watch them in Cúcuta. Asprilla didn't know where Cúcuta was before he got on the plane, but he scored two goals on his debut against Sergi Goycochea – the same goalkeeper who let in five goals to Colombia in Buenos Aires. The club offered him a house with no electricity and didn't pay him for three months.

I went to Cúcuta to find out more, but instead spent most of my brief stay having my travellers cheques rejected on account of new money-laundering laws. I lamented this to one bureau owner, whose name was Aparicio. Aparicio gave me a beer and was then joined by a man who produced a gun from inside his trousers. Aparicio handed him a box of bullets and he carefully loaded it. It was a beautiful silver thing and I imagined its cold barrel against my temple. I wanted very much to leave, but felt it would look rude after accepting the beer.

But the bullets weren't meant for me. The man left. 'If someone attacks you, you have to be able to defend yourself,' Aparicio explained. Many people carry guns in Colombia – especially wealthy people, which was the justification I was given for Asprilla's gun possession. I was quite shocked the time I saw several fellow guests at a rather high-class wedding produce handguns from inside their tuxedos to deal with some gatecrashers.

Aparicio gave me another beer and then took me around town. We drove past a recently car-bombed office. I found somewhere to get money and then his brother Mario took me to the airport on his motorbike, where we had more beers and exchanged tokens of friendship. He gave me his health insurance card. I gave him my leisure centre pass. Cúcuta was strange.

Asprilla was sold within a year to the Medellín club Atlético Nacional, the only Colombian club to win the premier South American competition, the Copa Libertadores. Pablo Escobar supported Nacional; Andrés Escobar played for them. Asprilla was signed partly on the recommendation of journalist Camilo Sixto Baquero, whom I met when I went to see Nacional play Junior at Medellín's Anastasio Girardot stadium. 'I told the Nacional president he was worth having a look at,' Sixto Baquero told me. 'He was still clumsy, rough around the edges. In Cúcuta they hardly paid him and he was starving – his mother had to send him money to buy food. He ate anything that was put in front of him when he came to Nacional. But there wasn't another player like him in Colombia. He was like a gazelle, so quick.'

The stadium was full of plaques, commemorating the 25th anniversary of the building of the stadium; the 50th anniversary of the building of the stadium; the visit of the Pope. There is also one to commemorate a free kick scored in one important game by René Higuita. Higuita is the goalkeeper whose 'scorpion kick' at Wembley in 1995 caused the crowd to dissolve into laughter. Today he was captaining Nacional. After only five minutes he came up to take a free kick on the edge of the Junior box. Nacional missed more clear chances than I have ever seen a football team miss and still won 3-0.

Asprilla had 'two brilliant years' at Nacional, said Sixto Baquero. He met his wife, Catalina, then 16, through connections at the club. But Asprilla, whose ambition had always been to play for Nacional, was a young man with money in his pocket in an exciting city. 'Medellín women are very friendly,' said Sixto Baquero, 'Asprilla is really quite timid.' After some talking-tos from club officials Asprilla got his mind on playing football.

In 1991, when Asprilla was playing for Nacional, his best friend from childhood shot himself aged 23. 'It destroyed me,' Asprilla has said.

He talked of giving up football, but signed for Parma, in Italy, in 1992, since when he has been Colombia's only constant presence in European football. Virtually every other player to have gone to Europe has been an unhappy failure. Freddy Rincón disappeared without trace at Napoli and Real Madrid. Adolfo Valencia, another black player from the backwards Pacific coast who was on the scoresheet that night in Buenos Aires, endured Teutonic hell at Bayern Munich (where his Christian name cannot have helped); he was soon offloaded to Atlético Madrid and was then shoved on loan to a succession of unglamorous outposts. Even Carlos Valderrama, a truly great player who was South American footballer of the year in 1987 before he led the exodus, underachieved at Montpellier and Valladolid. So he went back to Colombia and was the continent's footballer of the year again in 1993.

One journalist told me this record of failure was because most Colombian players were poorly educated. 'Alexis Mendoza has a degree,' he said, 'But most did not have much schooling. In the whole of Colombian football there are only about two or three doctors.' I pointed out there were not many doctors in English football either. Still, he insisted, your average Colombian player did not have the education of, say, his Argentinian contemporary, who can integrate in Europe more easily.

Asprilla does not have much education either, but unlike Valencia and Valderrama, who are renowned for being withdrawn, he is outgoing – which is partly why he has ended up in so many scrapes – and so makes friends. And as he has endured in Europe, everyone told me, he has matured. 'Now he's grown up too much,' said Sixto Baquero. 'He's more serious, more responsible, more conscious of what it means to live abroad, to live in different cultures. He has learned to live quietly, that you can't live out your private life in public.'

★ ★ ★

Colombia do not play their home games in the capital, Bogotá. Instead they have adopted Barranquilla, a coastal city of tropical languor, as their base. It is a welcoming city. Gabriel García Márquez once lived in a brothel here. Outside the Dann, the nondescript suburban hotel where the players were staying before flying off to Paraguay for the World Cup game, a banner strung across the street said: 'The Colombian squad is here'. So were a lot of military police.

I spent three days in Barranquilla and did as the large body of Colombian journalists did – hung about the hotel lobby in search of someone, anyone, to talk to. I gave four radio interviews. Each morning and afternoon the players would appear in the lobby in their football kit – it must be nice to be able to walk around luxury hotels in your football boots – and would try to spend as little time as possible with journalists and fans before climbing into the bus which took them to training. Then we would climb into our rickety cars and jeeps and chug off in pursuit of the bus to the training ground, where we would wait for things to happen. Once a pop star, Jorge Oñate, turned up, so everyone interviewed him. It was 8 a.m. and he looked as if it was a bit early for him. Another time one of the coaches walked over and said: 'Can't trust you folk round here with anything.' Someone had stolen some of goalkeeper Miguel Calero's kit. Calero appeared for breakfast the next day in his swimming trunks.

Asprilla is normally the last player to appear on the pitch, and he was invariably the last to show up to the bus – socks rolled down, mobile phone in hand, no sign of any football boots but with his feet stuffed into sandals. His standard expression was the familiar scared, 'don't hit me' one, as if he were about to cry. After training, while fans and press clustered around, Asprilla would be one of the first back on the bus.

Asprilla seems to be granted a large degree of leeway within the Colombian squad. On the first morning I watched training, while the rest of the players began their warm-up, Asprilla sat on the treatment table looking pained. But as soon as a camera crew came over to talk to him, he went over to join in the game. That lasted two seconds – literally. Then he went to have a play fight with one of the coaching staff. 'He's being difficult,' said the TV crew's reporter. 'He says he's got a headache.'

The next day Asprilla was still apparently troubled by some sort of mysterious injury. He lay on the treatment table, with the sporting director of the Colombian Football Federation, Gustavo Moreno Jaramillo, stroking his head and rubbing his ear. Asprilla finally got off the treatment table and wandered over for a chat with the coaches. He still didn't have his boots on. Then as the players all sat gathered around the coaching staff, apparently taking instructions, Asprilla got up and walked off, vainly pursued by his friend, goalkeeper Farid Mondragón, and Moreno Jaramillo. Leaving his boots behind, he walked out of the stadium. The training session went on, culminating in a long chat in the centre circle, the players lazing around with towels round their necks. It looked like a public show of bonding. Finally they went off laughing to the team bus, where Asprilla had been sitting by himself for nearly an hour.

The Colombia coach, Hernán Darío Gómez, played down the incident. He plays down everything with Asprilla. Asprilla played under Gómez at Nacional before he went to Italy, and the two, outwardly chalk and cheese, have a fine chemistry. Gómez, portly and moustachioed, told me himself that they were like father and son. In 1993, when Asprilla walked out of the Hotel Dann after being dropped from the team, and was told he would never play for Colombia again, it was Gómez who got him reinstated.

When I asked Gustavo Moreno Jaramillo about Asprilla, the first words he said were: 'He's mad.' Then he thought a bit more. 'He brightens up the whole team. Before he arrived we were all glum. Now he's here and he puts everyone in a good mood.' When the squad met up before the previous game, he told me, Asprilla sang in the lobby of the hotel.

'Asprilla bought a heart machine, in 1993, for the children's hospital in Barranquilla,' one journalist told me. 'He just wrote a cheque out in the lobby of the hotel here. He gave it to a nun. I was here when he gave her the cheque. It was at half past two,' he added.

There was also much speculation about the divorced Asprilla's relationship with a Colombian actress and model named Lady Noriega, the mention of whom induced much blowing out of cheeks and jealous shaking of heads among most men I talked to. Lady Noriega had just released a pop record which had been well received. She looked quite a fierce cat. In one magazine she was included in a list of Colombia's worst dressed women of 1997, pictured in a spotted fur three-piece ensemble of jacket, trousers and push-up bra. 'Personifies the worst nightmares of Cruella de Vil,' was the expert's judgement. 'A Dalmatian in a bra!' One man I met went very misty-eyed at the mention of her. 'We saw her once in a nightclub in Cancún, with a skirt up to here,' he said, indicating the level of his crotch. 'We felt very patriotic. Then at about five in the morning she went off with one of the bartenders.' Lady Noriega has apparently visited Asprilla in Newcastle, though presumably she packed something warmer than the dog outfit.

In Barranquilla I kept asking Asprilla for a chat but it was generally 'later' or 'tomorrow'. I finally managed to speak to him on the eve of Good Friday. Earlier I had accompanied his teammate Anthony De Avila and a television crew to the nearest church, where De Avila spent some time in positions of Catholic devotion for the benefit of the cameras, gawped at by several hundred fellow adherents. De Avila is strongly religious; when he played for América, the Cali club whose shirt badge depicts a devil, he covered up the badge before playing.

De Avila, a quiet, amenable man, now plays for New York Metro Stars in the United States. 'It's a very English style,' he said, wrinkling his nose. 'The ball's in the air the whole time.' De Avila is about five foot four.

We needed a police escort back to the hotel, where De Avila struck up a conversation with a pair of evangelical Protestants. A few minutes later Asprilla and Mondragón were dragged over to their table, one of the evangelicals saying: 'There's a lady here who would like a word with you.' It was obvious they were being summoned for some spiritual guidance. The group sat deep in conversation for some time, and bowed heads in prayer.

So by the time I asked Asprilla for a few words he was perhaps dwelling on spiritual matters, or just pissed off; certainly a few words were all I got. Yes, he liked it at Newcastle, where he was able to live very quietly; no, it was not so different from Italy. It didn't matter that he didn't get the chance to get back to Colombia much – he could relax and ride his horses in the holidays. I had thought he would feel like a fish out of water at Newcastle, but evidently not. 'I don't need to be surrounded by Latins to feel happy. What is important is what happens on the pitch. That's what I'm employed for,' he explained. And that was about it before he got up to head for the lifts. I barely had time to ask him about the little cameo I had just seen. Was religion important to him? He nodded sagely. 'It's always important to pray,' he said. 'Especially on a day like this.'

So I asked the two evangelicals about their meeting. 'I saw you praying with Faustino Asprilla – I didn't know he was very religious.'

One of them looked darkly at me. 'He's not,' she said rather shortly.

'What did you say to him?' I asked the other one.

'I told him that, yes, he has his money and fame, but fame will disappear,' she replied. 'But God is forever, and I told him he should remember that.'

I had planned to watch the Colombia game on TV in a clamorous bar surrounded by opinionated fans. In the event the only place I could find was a Chinese restaurant, where three boys and I watched over the shoulders of the Chinese owners, who were having dinner. I wore my Newcastle shirt. Before the game there was an item suggesting Carlos Valderrama should run for president. It showed a mock-up of Valderrama wearing the presidential sash. I don't *think* it was serious. Later there was a piece about the 70th birthday of Hungarian footballer Ferenc Puskas, illustrated entirely with library footage of Bob Paisley. The mistake was understandable – Paisley's tracksuit certainly looked as if it was the product of an Eastern European five-year plan.

Paraguay's only practice game had been cancelled when their opponents, a team in the Paraguayan first division, failed to turn up, but they did not seem unduly hindered. They scored after five minutes when Hugo Galeano deflected a cross into his own goal. A weeping Valderrama caricature walked across the screen, like the duck during the cricket on Australian TV. Colombia then had most of the game and Valderrama hit the bar. Asprilla was denied three times by Paraguay's goalkeeper, Jose Luis Chilavert.

With about five minutes left in the second half things got complicated. Asprilla and Chilavert clashed off the ball in the penalty area. Asprilla was sent off. Then Chilavert was sent off too and Colombia were awarded a penalty. Asprilla went to sit on the Colombia bench. Chilavert followed him over and spat on him. So Victor Aristizábal, who had already been substituted, got off the bench and launched a karate kick at Chilavert. So the riot police waded in. Then Valderrama almost started fighting with his teammate, Mondragón, who was trying to restrain him. The commentator had earlier predicted 'a ferocious battle in midfield', but it was turning into a ferocious battle off the field.

After about ten minutes of fascinating mayhem the match resumed with the penalty for Colombia. Mauricio Serna, who had missed a penalty against Argentina in the previous game, stood over the ball. Colombia held its breath. Serna, to his own evident relief, scored. The Valderrama cartoon performed a handspring across the screen and pulled his shirt over his head à la Ravanelli. We jumped about, except for the Chinese. Fireworks were set off outside. Colombia were heading for a very satisfying result that would keep them top of the group.

Then two minutes later, Mondragón missed a cross and Paraguay scored a soft winner.

Colombia was the country which spawned the legend of El Dorado, which has come to symbolise a fevered and fruitless quest for wealth and esteem. There is a lake at Guatavita, near Bogotá, where a Muisca Indian chieftain, coated in gold dust, was immersed each year in a ritual celebration of his power. When the Spanish *conquistadores* came they sent out expeditions to the interior to search for the source of these fabulous riches. The Indians soon worked out that the best way to get rid of the invaders was to tell them El Dorado was just round the next corner. This way the Spanish got lost, discovered the entire continent, and died of syphilis. When the lake at Guatavita was drained, there was nothing to be found.

Four hundred years later Colombians are trying to find their own El Dorado, a promised land away from murder and mayhem; perhaps even a land which the rest of the world does not instantly associate with cocaine. The place does not want to despair – it wants something to be proud of. Why not football?

Few people think of Brazil as a place where the police kill street kids, after all.

You only have to watch the news to know how much hope is invested in sport. 'Today Colombia wakes up saddened by the defeat of the national team – also by the problems in the rest of the country,' said the TV the day after the Paraguay game. The football led the news. Next up was a piece about a band of suspected burglars being shot dead during an attempted break-in in Bogotá. Other 'problems' included guerrilla skirmishes in several regions. During the build-up to the World Cup in 1994, the Colombian squad's visit to Disneyland was deemed more important than the mayor of one town being implicated in the murder of nine peasants.

The night Colombia beat Argentina 5-0, the country went mad; it was said about 50 people died in the celebrations which followed. Three months after that, Pablo Escobar was shot on a roof in Medellín, and things seemed set for a new era. The World Cup could not come quickly enough. Pelé tipped them to win.

And of course everyone knows what happened. 'A thorn lodged in the players' hearts,' I was told in Cali. Aparicio, my friend with the bureau de change in Cúcuta, put it best. '*Nos mata la grandeza*,' he said. 'Greatness kills us.' It has killed most players to have gone abroad, and it killed again in 1992 when a Colombian Under-23 team including Asprilla went to the Barcelona Olympics among the favourites, lost to Spain and Egypt, and only managed to draw with Qatar. Yet somehow everyone thought it would be different in 1994.

Before the 1994 World Cup Asprilla told his biographer Daniel Samper – the brother of the Colombian president – that he would retire after the competition and return to Tuluá, surrounded by horses and cattle, with time for a spot of fishing and his own football pitch. He was tired of the pressure of professional football. 'Anything I don't do in this World Cup, I'll never do,' he said. 'I'll be watching the 1998 World Cup from the stands.'

I reminded Asprilla of his planned retirement in Barranquilla, but he looked at me as if I'd just made it up. How could any of them retire after 1994? 'They want to go out by the front door, with their heads held high,' I was told in Cali. Alexis Mendoza and Carlos Valderrama will be 36 in France in 1998 – a lot older than Andrés Escobar would have been. Asprilla was a good friend of Escobar.

'Riot as Tino Sees Red', said Newcastle's *Evening Chronicle*, which I saw when I got back to England. Asprilla apparently 'completed his 15,000-mile round trip in disgrace'. I completed mine exhausted.

The week after the Paraguay game I went down to Newcastle's training ground in Durham. Training sessions attract hundreds of spectators who are kept in order by men like nightclub bouncers. Every arriving car is keenly scanned for signs of footballers. 'That looks like Shaka's car,' said a lad of about eight.

'What's Tino drive?' I asked.

'A Toyota.'

'Really?'

'I don't know.'

'They all get company cars,' said the lad's grandfather. 'One of them wrapped his round a lamppost the day he got it.'

'Ginola drives a Range Rover,' offered the young lad.

'They say that Elliott's wrapped three up,' said his grandfather. 'Three of them!'

Ginola turned up in a Renault.

The players came out for training. Some said, apropos of Darren Peacock: 'He's the one with one leg shorter than the other.' It was difficult to tell.

Asprilla came out with Les Ferdinand and a new signing called Des Hamilton – three black players together. Asprilla was having a play fight with Ferdinand. Ferdinand was laughing. Asprilla, who apparently sits on the team bus with a blanket over his head and listens to salsa, is a very popular player at Newcastle. 'He bridges the gap at the club between the Geordie lads – Lee Clark, Robbie Elliott – and the glamour boys like Les or David,' I was told. 'When they do go for a night out in a big group, Tino is always there.'

Throughout training Asprilla looked a lot more relaxed than he had in Barranquilla. He didn't even hurry off the pitch first at the end. One man nodded at Asprilla. 'Can you imagine him being any bother?' he said incredulously. 'They keep on saying he started a riot, he's a gun-toter, he's a drug smuggler – but everyone just wants to cuddle him.'

The only good *crónica roja* about Asprilla in Newcastle was in the *Sunday Sun*, the Newcastle-based tabloid, in May 1996. 'Asprilla Trashed my Villa', it revealed, before going on to recount a 'wrecking spree'; thousands of pounds of damage caused during an end-of-season party at his rented house in Northumberland. But Nick Emmerson, who was at the party, told me the account was exaggerated. Indeed the following week's paper had 'soccer pals' setting the record straight. Asprilla had tried to hide his cassettes in the hostess trolley but a guest had switched it on; he'd tried to light the fire but had ended up filling the house with smoke and soot. It painted a rather endearing picture of Asprilla as a hapless bachelor. 'He always kept his CDs in the hostess trolley,' said Emmerson, who was Asprilla's interpreter for six months before Asprilla was given an English teacher (he has apparently also been seen with an electronic translating machine). 'Some of them melted.'

After the 'villa-wrecking' incident Asprilla went to live in

Woolsington, which is about as close as you can get to New-castle Airport without having landing lights down your drive. David Ginola lived there too. It is a very small village composed almost entirely of very big houses, with intimidating signs marked 'private road' and 'Neighbourhood Watch'. I was just leaving when I spotted an elderly black man wearing a baseball cap shambling down the road. There are not many people like that in Woolsington – in fact not in the entire North East of England – so it was a fair bet this was one of Tino's house guests. It turned out to be his father.

Diego Asprilla proved a much more engaging conversation-alist than his son. Standing at Woolsington's bus stop in his Minnesota Wolverines baseball cap, open shirt, gold accessories, shabby beige slacks, and trainers, he looked completely Colom-bian and faintly bewildered, as if he had fallen asleep on the bus from Tuluá, ended up somewhere he did not recognise, and was now trying to find his way back, without realising he was not just six but six thousand miles off course.

Diego used to be an amateur footballer with his factory team (*el Rápido*, they called him) and the more we talked about football, the more animated he became. He rolled his eyes talking about Les Ferdinand's performance against Sunderland the previous Saturday. 'Oh, he missed a *stack* of sitters!' he said. 'You have got to shoot like this, to the side—' and here he danced about, firing imaginary balls past an invisible Sunder-land goalkeeper, '—to the left, or the right. But he hit them straight at his belly button. You only get a few chances and you have to make them count. That's what Paraguay did against Colombia.' We agreed that Ferdinand lacked guile and compo-sure, and that Newcastle's midfield needed strengthening for the next season. ('More support for Faustino. More Colombian-style players.')

Diego likes and admires England. He spends a lot of time

here with his son – not in the winter, though – and enjoys wandering about, popping to Tesco up the road, and getting amused looks when he hands over his credit card. He thinks it is a place where people respect each other. 'This is such a disciplined country. Look at this,' he said, pointing at the few cars passing by. 'Everyone drives correctly, on the proper side of the road! And I can go out with my watch and my wallet, and not worry about getting robbed.' I was touched to find someone so obviously Anglophile. 'It will take Colombia 200 years to catch up with London!' he predicted.

As for Faustino, there is something of the urchin in him which complements Newcastle. Emmerson said: 'He is always going to the Metro Centre. He loves playing in the arcades. That video game where you sit on a motorbike? That's his favourite. He plays with all the little Geordie lads who are skiving school. He'll give one of them a fiver and tell him to go and get him some change. Then when the kid comes back he'll give him a pound and they'll play in the arcades.

'The Metro Centre is his favourite place. He is very impressed by material things and by wealth, definitely. We went to Singapore and he bought a Rolex, but he didn't wear it. He just carried it around in this crappy little bum bag, just because he liked it.'

When Asprilla lived in Italy he used to like going fishing. 'When he first came he wanted to get a fishing boat,' said Emmerson. 'So they took him to Tynemouth the first weekend he was here. He took one look at the North Sea and said, "Fuck that!" He has never mentioned it again.'

And some things about Newcastle evidently baffle him. On their first night out together, Emmerson told me, he took Asprilla to Newcastle's Quayside, a strip of pubs and clubs. 'I said to Tino, "You are not going to believe the lasses and what they are wearing – bra tops and miniskirts." It was snowing and he had this big fur overcoat on, and he said yeah, yeah, like he didn't believe me. Anyway we went out and straight away this lass saw us and shouted "Tino!" and turned round and flashed her arse at him, she just had this little G-string on. And he just said, "¡*Vaya ciudad!*" ' What a town!

In the centre of Newcastle is a fruit-and-veg stall called the Toon Barra, painted black and white and adorned with portraits of great players of past and present, with their autographs. Asprilla is already there. It could be the first time he has been asked to sign a market stall. The barrow also shows the 'Dream Team' – Keegan, Terry McDermott and Sir John Hall.

The Toon Barra, if it hasn't been changed since I last saw it, is out of date. Kenny Dalglish became Newcastle manager when Keegan resigned early in 1997. Since then the fun has gone out of the place. At the training ground – which it is said Dalglish wants to make less accessible to the public – one autograph hunter was collecting signatures on her team strip. 'If it's Kenny Dalglish,' she said, pointing to the hem at the bottom, 'I'm going to get him to sign it down here, 'cos I hate him.'

Even if Dalglish wins the championship ten years on the trot, it is difficult to imagine him being seen in the same light as Keegan. The difference is in style. Towards the end of the 1995–96 season, when Newcastle were desperately trying to cling to their title ambitions, the team played Liverpool in a league match and lost 4-3 in what was described as the game of the decade. Asprilla scored Newcastle's third, meeting a through ball in his stride with the outside of his right foot, and sending it past the Liverpool goalkeeper and curling in towards the goal. Nick Emmerson told me: 'Tino was amazed about scoring three goals at Liverpool and still losing. He just couldn't understand how it could happen, that you could score three goals away from home against a team third in the championship and still lose.'

I was in a bar in Newcastle watching the same fixture on television this year, with Dalglish now the manager. We were off the league pace, and desperately needed a win to keep us, however remotely, in the championship hunt. Newcastle were dreadful. Asprilla was playing up front by himself, normally at least 30 yards from his nearest teammate. Newcastle had their other ten players in their own half. Occasionally they would try to pass to Asprilla, who would chase gamely and fail to get the ball. Usually they passed it among themselves until they gave it away to Liverpool. Warren Barton seemed not to know what to do. At half-time it was 3-0 and Newcastle had not even had a shot on goal.

'This is the worst twatting performance I have seen in my life!' said one of the group to my right.

There were injury problems, true. But Dalglish could have picked Ginola, pushed Beardsley up to help Asprilla, taken Liverpool on. At half-time Ginola and the semi-fit Ferdinand were lined up to come on. There was a big cheer. Ferdinand lasted ten minutes, and contributed one header, Newcastle's first effort on goal, before he went off again.

Then after 70 minutes Gillespie scored a soft goal with a shot from the edge of the area. There were ironic cheers. 'One goal from two shots! That's championship form!' said someone.

But the ghost of Keegan stirred. After 87 minutes Ginola swept a long crossfield pass and Asprilla, virtually at the same spot on the pitch from where he had scored last year, dipped a lob over James. There was an agonising moment when it seemed to be going wide and then suddenly it was in the corner of the net.

The bar went daft. One wag remembered Keegan. 'I will love it if we beat them, love it!' he screamed. The rest was inevitable, pure Keegan. Two minutes later, as Liverpool panicked, Asprilla challenged for the ball in the box and it broke to

Warren Barton, Newcastle's most vilified player of the evening, who scored the equaliser. Someone said: 'Watch where you're throwing your dregs!' But I knew what was going to happen. Liverpool scored. In injury-time, just as they had in 1996. 4-3. The bar went silent. You thought of the often-replayed image of Keegan the year before, slumped on the advertising hoardings.

'I will love it if we beat them, love it!' was Keegan's outburst as the title race with Manchester United drew to a close. He knew that Newcastle was looking for El Dorado. It does not have guerrillas or narcoterrorists, but a lot of bad things have happened to the city. People now bring coal to Newcastle, while not many people build ships there. So we turn football into a matter of pride, and queue to buy replica shirts in their thousands as soon as they go on sale at midnight.

Newcastle were leading the Premiership by nine points, and had played a game less than their rivals, when Asprilla signed. They had it at their feet; and Asprilla, his country's most successful football ambassador, had a chance to make Britain think Colombia was something other than controversial or enigmatic, to make up for 1994. He made his home debut against Manchester United, the team in second place, when Newcastle had won all of their previous 13 home games. Asprilla played well. Newcastle lost 1-0. Greatness kills us.

When the championship was finally lost on the last day of the season, many people blamed the introduction of Asprilla. 'If he bought a newspaper he would ask me what it said,' said Nick Emmerson. 'Sometimes I was selective.' But the next season his name still got one of the loudest cheers at St James' Park.

I think this is because Asprilla, more than anyone else, epitomises the Keegan era. Employing Asprilla was an act of faith on Keegan's part; an explicit indication of his footballing philosophy. Keegan wore his heart on his sleeve and every

Newcastle fan could see he was also embarked on a fevered quest for El Dorado, a dreamed-of land where titles could be won by teams that played with more attackers than defenders. We went along with it, and when Asprilla beat Steve Vickers in his first game at Middlesbrough, it seemed we would get there. Now, when the promised land has dissolved into a desert mirage, I think we still go along with it. We would rather keep searching and hope that one day we might stumble across that lake, shimmering in the evening light, full of gold.

'rally round you havens!': soccer and the literary imagination

D . J . TAYLOR

This need for tribal identity applies particularly to football – a puerile game, by any rational measure, but one
that elicits powerful emotions from grown men. True,
you will find intellectuals who 'support' one team or
another, but this is a symbol, perhaps, of the bourgeois'
confusion about his identity. He searches for a tribe to
alleviate his sense of alienation.

Piers Paul Read, *Knights of the Cross* (1997)

It is a Saturday afternoon, let us say, in February 1971 and I am
ten years old. The place is a three-quarter size football pitch in
the grounds of Blackdale School on the outskirts of south-west
Norwich, and the occasion a match between the 14th Norwich
Cubs and, it might be, the 27th Norwich or the 19th Norwich, or
any other ornament of the Bobby Charlton division of the local
cub scout league. Twenty-six years on, I can recall this scene
with a rather ominous particularity. Grey mist, rolling up from
the Cringleford marshes, hangs low over the field, partly obscur-
ing the 20 or 30 spectators (a select contingent which includes
my father and two Dickensian characters named Mr Moss and
Mr Downes who 'manage' the side) and causing the shouts and
cries 50 yards away to echo from a kind of netherworld of dim
figures and shadowy half-light. Even in the curiously hairy
knee-length shorts that my mother makes me wear in preference

to the flimsy items handed out to the other boys, it is stupendously cold.

What happens? After about ten minutes the ball trickles out from some midfield scrimmage to the remote, unmarked position I occupy on the extreme left-hand touchline and I collect it on my toe. A half-back emerges tentatively out of the mist, but I flick the ball carefully to one side of him and then tear over his outstretched leg away down the left wing. I'm a big lad for ten (sadly in a couple of years I'll return to average height and weight) and I can sprint 100 metres in 15 seconds. The full-back, a scared looking nine-year-old, divines something of this superiority as he approaches and shies away with only the briefest attempt to engage. Just the goalkeeper to beat. To the right of the goalpost I can see my father mouthing something, almost certainly the words 'far post'. Five yards out now, I decide to ignore this exemplary piece of advice. Finding the ball still stuck miraculously to my left foot – there have been occasions when in my anxiety to score I've hared off down the wing with this vital accessory becalmed in a divot – I simply blast it straight at the keeper, a lymphatic ten-year-old who sinks imploringly to his knees as the net billows behind him. The last thing I see is my father's hands raised above his head in exaltation.

I don't suppose the foregoing happened exactly as described even once, but something like it undoubtedly took place a great many times on that far-off Elysian field. The 14th had a good season in 1970–71. According to the press cuttings snipped from the *Norwich Mercury* I looked out the other night – an unnecessary act as my memory of the statistics was accurate to the last digit – our record was P 17, W 16, D 0, L 1, F 152, A 13, Pts 32. And 43 of that majestic goals-for total were contributed by my left foot. What happened next? That summer I turned eleven, left the cubs for the scouts and moved from Norwich School's preparatory department to the main school, where you played rugby in the autumn and hockey in the spring, and, with the exception of a few mid-twenties appearances for an outfit named the Captain Scott Invitation XI (its summer incarnation is memorialised in Marcus Berkmann's wonderful cricket book *Rain Men*), never set foot on a soccer pitch again. Needless to say, I still have my championship medal, and although I don't propose to bore you with them, I can still remember the other ten names on the team-sheet.

On the face of it, football – one of the things that regularly annoys me about memoirs of bygone public school life is a habit of referring to 'football' when the author means 'rugby' – ought to provide a perfect subject for fiction. There are several reasons for this, but one of the more obvious is that it involves at least 22 people spending 90 minutes in the same place, leaving aside the pre-and post-match socialising. Another is the game's centrality (along with boxing, pop music and organised crime) to the whole notion of working-class self-advancement, a social phenomenon in which the twentieth-century English novel has occasionally shown some mild interest. Then there is the agreeable, if sometimes faintly insidious, way in which soccer can transform itself into a moral exercise – the rock-like defender humbled by the jinking imp, the non-League club that brings down the Premiership's finest, that whole motivational dynamic of doing one's best against insuperable odds. Finally, and in some ways uniting the previous explanations into a single point of focus, there is the fact that soccer is essentially a *romantic* activity. To explain this attraction I can only go back to the pitch at Blackdale School, with my father standing on the touchline. As a child the highlight of my life – better than coming top of the form (which I did with unfailing regularity), better than the friskiest diversion or treat – was scoring those goals. Part of it was to do with sheer sensation – acres of green grass, the goal looming towards you, the rictus of agony on the keeper's face; a bit more, perhaps, to do with the tremendous detonation of confidence that sporting prowess brings to a ten-year-old (miraculously, scoring a hat-trick *actually made you popular*, whereas top marks in French simply meant a compass point jabbed in your leg). There was even – and even as a child I think I appreciated a little of this – the scent of class, or rather of a social divide momentarily transcended, in that I lived in a four-bedroomed house in a middle-class suburb and went to prep school while the rest of the team mostly dwelt in council houses on the West Earlham estate.

Human contact. Class. Moral combat. *Romance*. Ideal materials for producing a novel, you might think. And yet amid the great mass of sporting literature thrown up in the last century or so, decent creative writing about soccer scarcely exists. In a lifetime – I am 36 – spent reading soccer literature, I don't suppose I've come across more than half-a-dozen novels that managed to be 'about' soccer while still retaining some faint validity as works of art. Perhaps, to be fair, it is merely that the wrong kind of criteria are being applied. Most of the great 'sporting novels', if it comes down to it, are only 'about' sport in the most peripheral sense, cricket or golf (predominantly cricket) supplying a venue on which a particular set of moral problems can be dramatically enacted. Frederick Exley's *A Fan's Notes*, to take a classic example, might be described as an anatomy of American drunkenness which happens to take place in the vicinity of some baseball stadia. In David Storey's *This Sporting Life*, on the other hand, the quarry trailed across the pitted landscapes of professional rugby league is working-class identity. Even J.L. Carr's *A Season in Sinji*, which is sometimes spoken of as the greatest cricket novel ever written, is largely a story of personal conflict – two officers on a Second World War RAF outstation who quarrel over a girl –

given definition and context by the sporting backdrop.

To make this point, perhaps, is only to restate an axiom about any sort of creative writing: in the end, physical activity of any kind can only be secondary to what goes on in the characters' heads – a link in the chain of plot, or occasionally simple authorial self-indulgence (think of the number of times a Trollope novel is suddenly broken up by a hunting sketch). At the same time writing effectively about soccer presents an aesthetic problem to the writer that is less conspicuous in writing about, say, cricket or trout-fishing. One can see this on the occasions when a journalist in one of the Sunday news-papers decides to pull out all the stops, the better to describe some titanic mêlée between the goalposts. Carr's *How Steeple Sinderby Wanderers Won The FA Cup* – of which more later – contains a witheringly accurate send-up of this kind of elevated reportage, in the shape of an account of a cup final by *The Times'* 'Nigel Kelmscott-Jones':

> The wretched McClusky advanced from his goal, retreated, advanced again and when the majestic shot came, leapt hopelessly in the wrong direction. It struck the crossbar like a thunderclap. Then, as it bounced back, Wembley exploded. Those that sat stood. Those that stood leapt. McClusky scrambles back to his line, Slingsby comes in at great speed, takes the ball on his chest, controls, steadies it and hammers it into the pit of the goalman's stomach. And he, wrapped up like a parcel, collapses into the back of the net, guiltily trying to detach the ball from his person.

This is a joke, of course, but the chances of finding something like it in this week's *Sunday Telegraph*, or hearing it in one of Stuart Hall's Radio Five Live broadcasts, would be fairly high.

Somehow writing about soccer in the supercharged purple prose of the up-market cricket book (the Cardus–Arlott kind, in which boundaries are invariably 'sweetly struck' or, if the chap really fancies himself, even 'smote') seems fantastically inappropriate, if only because of the blatant distance between medium and thing described. A useful comparison, perhaps, is with fictional accounts of sex. Sex, as conceived by the average novelist, is again a romantic activity. Yet the sexual act itself comes hedged about with any number of unromantic physical details. Given liberal orthodoxies about 'frankness' and 'seeing things as they are', nine novelists out of ten will want to find room for the physical detail, only to discover that in accommodating it they have lost sight of their original aim. The same, *mutatis mutandis*, is true of soccer: on the one hand an ideal of stalwart Corinthians valiantly defending e'en unto death; on the other a stark reality of embrocation, sore knees and the danger of being maimed by the opposing centre-back.

Naturally there are other reasons why it is difficult to write convincingly about 22 men chasing a ball. Another drawback might be the characteristic inarticulacy of the game's participants, which in fictional terms is the eternal problem of equating the sensibility of the artefact with that of the characters the author has chosen to populate it. Perhaps in the last resort this is just a way of saying that novels about soccer tend to be written by educated gentlefolk who have observed the game from afar while the cast of such works will necessarily be thick herberts, and that a certain amount of patronage, or rather distance between writer and raw material, is inevitable. As an example of the difficulties involved in this kind of writing, it is worth examining Hunter Davies' novel *Striker* (1992), the braggart and selective memoirs of 'Joe Swift', an agglomeration of real people with a passing resemblance to Paul Gascoigne (at any rate Joe is a Geordie who proceeds via Tottenham Hotspur to a lucrative career in Europe). To concentrate on *Striker*'s deficiencies is not to knock Hunter Davies, whose book about Spurs, *The Glory Game*, was a shrewd exposure of the old-style game, but to suggest one or two of the difficulties faced by a clever and observant man in writing about people who, by and large, are neither of these things and may even – this being a characteristic of business, which soccer has effectively turned itself into – be venal into the bargain.

The most striking thing, as it happens, about Davies' novel is its artificiality, or rather its relentless tongue-in-cheek quality. There are the jokes about other footballers, the managerial mutterings about 'daft as a brush' (the manager claims that he said 'we need Rush', as in Ian), even a series of fake letters from famous names – Garth Crooks, Graeme Souness, Bobby Robson – confirming or denying (mostly denying) incidents from the Swift mythology. This steady drip of insider wise-cracking reaches a torrent during a scene in the England dressing room – this is the early 1990s, remember – where Terry Butcher can be found glued to his Walkman and the real Gazza on the phone throwing money at his bookie. All this, perhaps, is at least plausible – all too plausible in one respect. The novel's central conceit, on the other hand, is the purest corn. At an early stage the reader becomes aware that Joe is writing the book under some kind of sequestration, that he is even being held captive in some way. It turns out that in the wake of the highly publicised transfer to Juventus he now finds him imprisoned in a remote Italian monastery, having been lifted by kidnappers. What we have in the end, however amusing to anyone in the know, is simply a piece of hokum, in which occasional nods in the direction of verisimilitude are always liable to be compromised by the gags, and the feeling that nearly everyone involved in the proceedings is the victim of the author's semi-indulgent patronage.

There must be better soccer novels than *Striker*. Where are they? Or why haven't they been written? One can start the search for an answer to these questions by taking a look at what might grandly be called the impact of soccer on the literary consciousness, by which I mean what writers thought about soccer when they found out about it and the kind of books that got written as a result.

The emergence of soccer as an integral part of English social life came in the late nineteenth century. Although early FA Cup finals tended to be won by amateur sides made up of public school old boys, the game was essentially a working-class amusement, whose popularity was to have a revolutionary effect on the national fabric. It is not being fanciful, for example, to trace a connection between the rise of soccer, or rather its symbolic presence at the head of a pageant of working-class leisure pursuits, and the decline of organised religion. The ecclesiastical historian David Newsome, examining the question of late-Victorian church attendance, suggests that 'the greatest threat of all was the diversion offered to all classes, and the lower classes most of all, by the advent of professional football. This is what the working man regarded as the highlight of his weekend.' To many representatives of the various national churches, Newsome concludes (in his 1997 study *The Victorian World Picture: Perceptions and Introspections in an Age of Change*) that it seemed as if the passion engendered by football was rapidly becoming the working man's religion. Prudently the church attempted to channel or to colonise some of this enthusiasm, and the distinguishing mark of the keen young early twentieth-century cleric was his willingness to sponsor church youth teams. As a fellow-clergyman observes of the aloof and octogenarian Canon Jocelyn in F.M. Mayor's *The Rector's Daughter* (1924), 'Playing soccer with the lads is since his day.'

Sooner or later, as with any social phenomenon, all this was likely to attract the attention of novelists. Predictably enough, the attitudes of those early twentieth-century writers who chanced upon the game were not so much hostile as merely uncomprehending. At bottom, this was a question of upbringing. The specimen novelist of the early part of this century was likely to have been educated at a minor public school: such sporting passions as he evinced were nearly always expended on cricket. Soccer, consequently, consisted of not much more than two groups of young men trying to kick each other. This attitude persisted until well into the middle of the century. Orwell's essay 'The Sporting Spirit', published in 1945 as a response to a recent tour of the UK by a Moscow Dynamo XI, and reprinted in his *Collected Essays, Journalism and Letters Volume IV* (1968), is a fair example of this incomprehension of the kind of feelings that soccer arouses – all the more so in that it is the work of an avowedly left-wing writer with a passionate interest in popular culture. Interested by the reports of bad feeling circulating at the tour's close (two players had apparently come to blows in the match against Arsenal, which seems pretty mild by today's standards), Orwell set out to examine 'how and why the modern cult of sport arose'. His conclusion, oddly enough, is that 'the whole thing is bound up with the rise of nationalism – that is, with the lunatic modern habit of identifying oneself with large power units and seeing everything in terms of competitive prestige'. As for the proposed return visit by a British XI, we ought to send a second-rate team which is sure to be beaten and cannot be claimed to represent Britain as a whole. 'There are quite enough real causes of trouble already, and we need not add to them by encouraging young men to kick each other on the shins amid the roars of infuriated spectators.'

It is queer that Orwell, so sane and sensible about practically everything else, should have such a blind spot about soccer. (If this sounds like sour grapes, I should say that Orwell means more to me than virtually any other twentieth-century English writer.) There are points to be made on both sides, of course. No doubt nationalism has infected the modern game – exhibit number one might be the England/Germany match in Euro 96. No doubt, too, for England to play Germany at soccer every so often is better than to have them fighting actual wars. At the same time, going back to the period at which Orwell was writing – around the end of the Second World War – my father was at the England/Hungary game of 1953, and his account of the game always touches on the collective awe of the Wembley crowd when faced with the superior skills of Puskas and Hidegkuti, rather than virulent irruptions of national spirit. But there is a terrific irony in the spectacle of a left-wing writer on the one hand confusing a genuine working-class leisure pursuit with an instrument of power politics, and on the other deliberately emphasising its more prosaic side ('encouraging young men to kick each other on the shins amid the roars of infuriated spectators').

In contrast to Orwell, other early twentieth-century writers have a habit of stressing the class aspects of soccer. P.G. Wodehouse's *Mike and Psmith* (1910), for instance, is one of the first novels to hint at the way in which soccer had begun to colonise the national terrain. Wodehouse was of course a cricket fanatic, an allegiance later transferred to golf: his hero, fresh-faced Mike Jackson, is a promising young batsman whose father's financial losses rob him of a place at Cambridge. Incarcerated in a city bank, and providentially reunited with his old school-chum Psmith – Psmith *père* reckons his son needs a crash course in the real world – Mike's thraldom at the hands of daily routine is mitigated only when Psmith resolves to make an ally of their immediate superior, Mr Rossiter. He does this by feigning an interest in Manchester United, at one of whose

London games the starchy bank official has been seen. Much of this – Psmith, for instance, mugging up on the Edwardian equivalent of tabloid soccer gossip – is hugely funny, for all that Wodehouse's sympathies are clearly with desk-bound Mike (the novel's finale is an inspired description of his hastily arranged debut at Lord's). Soccer features as an outlandish ritual taking place beyond the normal confines of civilised life. Despite this habitual distancing, the atmosphere of *Mike and Psmith* is heavy with its scent. Mike's landlady, showing him round his dismal lodgings (prior to his removal to Psmith's bachelor flat), is described as dribbling a piece of fluff under the bed in the style of a professional footballer. Similarly, in a scene on Kennington Common where Mike squares up to a rough who has thrown a stone at mild-mannered Mr Waller – another of the bank's employees, who doubles up as a socialist orator – the first shout of a sporting onlooker is 'Ply up the Arsenal!'

Other pre- and post-Great War novelists were more flagrantly conscious of soccer's symbolic role in the class divide. *Sorrell and Son* (1925), Warwick Deeping's best-selling account of an impoverished ex-officer who takes a job as a hotel porter as a means of providing for his son, reaches one of its many figurative climaxes on a football pitch. Sorrell's initial impulse is to send his son to the local council school. Turning up to watch a school match he discovers that the boy, whom the urchins nickname 'Collars and Cuffs', is an object of derision. 'Sorrell saw his son "fouled" on more than one occasion, and the boys near him gloated and laughed, but when he showed legitimate spirit in a challenge or a tackle they snarled at him.' There follows a swift post-match exchange ('Do you like playing with those boys, Kit?' 'No – I don't, pater.') after which Sorrell scrapes together the money to send his son to a private school. His final injunction to the boy is to 'play hard – the big game, you know, our game, my son'. This is a moral exhortation rather than an instruction to take up rugby, but one can't help feeling that the two are somehow connected.

Some more family history. In the early 1930s my father attended the same school to which, 40 years later, I was sent myself. He did so in rather different circumstances – as the solitary scholarship boy on a sprawling West Norwich council estate. So far as I can judge, though he was happy enough to send his sons there, my father didn't particularly enjoy his time at Norwich School, then a grammar of ancient foundation, now an immensely successful private establishment. Of the many stories he tells about this five-year immersion in a chilly bath of class-consciousness, two stand out. The first concerns a sadistic schoolmaster named J.S. Redmayne – which may sound uncharitable to the dead, but no other word fits – whose amiable habit it was, first thing on a Monday morning, to toss a coin in front of the class and ask my father to call. If my father guessed wrong, Redmayne hit him. If on the other hand he guessed correctly Redmayne also hit him 'for looking pleased with himself' or some such nonsense. (After his death Redmayne had a playing field named after him, which may say something about the gap between official and unofficial history.) The second story takes in my father's first game of soccer (Norwich School was, and is, a rugger school but they let pre-teens play the round ball game). This took place on a picturesquely named bit of marshland called Cow Meadow, near the river Wensum, under the benign superintendence of a character named Johnny Spence. According to my father's account, none of the other boys seemed to know very much about the manner in which the game was played. Consequently, having seized upon the ball from the kick-off, he merely dribbled it dextrously through a startled clump of defenders and smashed it past the goalkeeper. Having done this, and ignoring the indifferent stares of the bystanders, he looked around for some means of celebrating. A regular at Norwich City's home games at the Nest, and desperately emulous of contemporary heroes such as Jack Vinall, my father sprinted to the corner flag, sank to his knees and warmly embraced it. Whereupon he received the most terrific ticking off to the effect that this wasn't the kind of behaviour expected of Norwich Schoolboys and he could stop it *now*.

It would be foolish to exaggerate the symbolic properties of this incident. At the same time it would be equally wrong to pretend that soccer didn't somehow lurk in the background of my father's attitude to his schooldays, and vice versa. J.S. Redmayne, for example, was a rugger fanatic and made a point of using Norwich City's defeats as a prop in his Monday morning execrations. Undeniably, too, soccer played a part in the literary and by extension the moral influences to which my father was being exposed. Like many another teenager in the 1930s, he was a fan of boys' school stories – solid hardbacks, given as Christmas presents by friends and family, with titles like *Cousins at Carsdale* and *The Liveliest Term at Templeton*. The role played by these books in the life of the average pre-war adolescent was an odd one. As Orwell points out in his essay on 'Boys' Weeklies', discussing Frank Richards' Billy Bunter stories, such items, though purporting to describe life in an English public school, were neither aimed at nor read by public schoolboys. In reality they were directed a little – or a lot – lower down the social scale: an agreeable fantasy version of teenage life at 'Greyfriars', 'Carsdale' or wherever, devised for the edification of the lower-middle classes and beyond – people like my father, in fact. Such books were invariably, if implicitly, moral exercises, and the medium by which they conveyed their messages was very often soccer. No other factor, perhaps, so aptly illustrates the distance between the cheery atmosphere of the fictional public school and the reality that lay behind it. The majority of

English public schools in the inter-war years played rugby, and yet the compilers of stories got up to glorify their existence were uneasily aware that if they ignored soccer they would risk losing their potential, predominantly soccer-fancying audience. Perhaps – and their identities for the most are simply lost in time – they were soccer players themselves. Fortunately, school story writers of the 1920s and 1930s such as R.A.H. Goodyear and Herbert Hayens realised that, quite as much as rugby, soccer made an excellent vehicle for inculcating lessons about team spirit and playing the game, and that despite – or perhaps because of – its location in the culture of another class, it could also be used to make valuable points about class divisions.

Typically in boys' school stories soccer is the motivating force by which keen, purposeful boys revitalise shiftless houses or schools whose headmasters deplore their want of purpose and fibre. In R.A.H. Goodyear's *Strickland of the Sixth*, for example, moribund, inaccessible 'Havenhall' (located somewhere in Yorkshire, as far as one can make out from the local accent) has been watching its rolls decline for years. Strickland, the square-jawed school captain, resolves to put the place back on the map by entering a team for the local amateur cup. All this is accomplished in the face of considerable opposition from the snootier kind of soccer-hating sixth-former (there is a marvellous highbrow villain called 'Sark') and teachers aghast at the kind of low-class adversaries the XI will find itself up against. Predictably, in the circumstances, the novel comes dripping with class-consciousness (none of it, it should be said, particularly offensive – Goodyear's politics, so far as they can be inferred, seem to have been those of a well-meaning One Nation Conservative). This tendency reaches its height in the course of a first-round tie against a team of working-class apprentices going under the name of 'Asheltubla'. Narrowly beaten by a goal to nil, their last-minute appeals for a penalty turned down by an inflexible ref, the Tubs' baying supporters are in no doubt as to the cause of their defeat: 'Allus favouring them cos they're the sons of toffs!' The game ends with a pitch invasion and an attempted assault on the referee, forestalled by Strickland, the shouts of 'Rally round you Havens!' ringing in his ears, laying out the assailant with a well-aimed sock on the jaw.

Strickland of the Sixth is an interesting period piece – inverting the social basis of soccer to show a collection of upper-middle-class boys reading their working-class opponents a metaphorical lecture about 'team spirit' and 'fair play' (significantly, in the next round Havenhall play a much more respectful working-class team who accept their defeat like gentlemen). While the message (chaps showing oiks how to behave) is standard, the medium is not. The same kind of moral lesson, this time reflecting a different sort of class awareness, turns up in Herbert Hayens' *Play Up Kings!* (The *Play Up!* books, each of them focused on a particular sport, were immensely popular in the 1930s.) Here again a good-natured, morally 'sound' boy named Clarice is given the job of rejuvenating 'King's', a once great house now fallen on evil days. The problem, it soon turns out, is the clique assembled around one 'Marmaduke Howard', a florid, domineering snob who claims descent from the aristocratic family of that name but is actually the son of a Jewish war profiteer. Clarice's plan to restore some of the house's self-respect involves winning the inter-house soccer cup. Howard and Co.'s opposition to the scheme stems partly from the fact that Clarice is an interloper, but underlying it is the never quite openly expressed objection that playing soccer is 'vulgar'. As you may imagine, King's wins the cup. His social pretensions, ancestry and talent for blackmail having been pitilessly exposed, 'Marmy' leaves the school under a cloud.

Play Up Kings! shows the gentlemanly values of all for one and one for all being used to rebuke an aspiring moneyed class, the people who had 'done well out of the war', on the grounds that its members are morally unfit to sit down at an upper-middle-class table. Both novels, it should be said, combine exhortation of this sort with a good deal of energetic reportage of the 'With a mighty kick Strickland prevented what seemed a certain goal' kind, and *Strickland of the Sixth*, in particular, contains pages of high-class soccer reporting. However unquantifiable, the influence of this kind of reading material on two or three generations of twentieth-century schoolboys (I was still reading the books in the 1970s) cannot be ignored. It was scarcely surprising to find that on the occasion, late in my father's school career, when my grandfather was summoned to the place to have the headmaster diffidently enquire of him what my father proposed to 'do' in life, he should murmur something about training to be a sports journalist. It was even less surprising, however, to find that the headmaster pooh-poohed the suggestion entirely, and that my father ended up as an insurance clerk.

The typical school story of the 1930s – such things can be picked up for a few pence in any second-hand shop, and are well worth reading – was an odd mixture of romance and moralising. To find anything like a realistic description of the experience of attending or playing in a football match it's necessary to move on to the post-war era. A good example of the former is Alan Sillitoe's 'The Match' (included in his first collection *The Loneliness of the Long-distance Runner*, 1959) in which a cross-grained middle-aged man is raised to such an extremity of temper by watching Notts County lose at home that he quarrels irrevocably with his wife. The rise of the Angry Young working-class novelist of the 1950s and 1960s meant that there existed a number of writers to whom the social context of soccer and the sheer knowledge of what it was like to play it were not entirely divorced from personal experience, and the game provides a background to a fair amount of 1950s writing. But even some of Brian Glanville's early work, notably the well-known story 'Goalkeepers Are Crazy', or a piece like Bill Naughton's 'The Goalkeeper's Revenge', where the hero gets his own back on the arrogant professional centre-forward who snubbed him as a boy by humiliating him in a fairground penalty-taking competition, pale in comparison with David Storey's *This Sporting Life* (1960). Storey's novel is less a book about sport than a study of a personality, but his experience of playing professional rugby league allows a sharp whiff of authenticity to float across some of the on-field sequences, in particular the scene in which Arthur Makin, his ghastly protagonist, thumps an opponent in the scrum and contrives to pass the blame on to someone else.

If anything in soccer fiction comes close to *This Sporting Life*, it is a little-known novel by Gordon M. Williams called *From Scenes Like These* (1968) which despite its current obscurity – Williams doesn't appear in the recent *Reader's Companion to Twentieth Century Writers*, for instance – was shortlisted for the first Booker Prize. (Williams went on to write *The Siege of Trencher's Farm*, filmed as *Straw Dogs*, and co-authored some detective novels with Terry Venables before falling off the literary map.) Set in early 1950s Ayrshire, *From Scenes Like These* is, again, only parenthetically a football novel – on one level it can be read as an account of the decay of a particular kind of rural Scottish life – but soccer is central enough to the aspirations of its teenage hero to loom very large over the questions which the book sets out to answer. Duncan 'Dunky' Logan, Williams' hero, works on a farm whose outlying land is steadily being swallowed up by the sprawling township in which he lives. Unhappily lodged in a tenement flat with an exigent mother and a bed-bound father, interested in girls and

breeding rabbits and not averse to attending the odd Communist Party meeting, Dunky is avid to escape. Saturday afternoon games for the second XI of a West of Scotland League
side called Cartneuk, managed by a famous local talent-spotter
named Baldy Campbell, are a way out. 'Nobody ever knew
just how seriously you took it, how much you hoped that one
day you'd play a blinder and a strange man would come up to
you after the game and write your name down in a wee book
and ask you if you wanted a trial with Rangers or Aston Villa
or Leicester City. Or even Ayr United – he wasn't fussy.'
Williams' method of describing the games is an odd, split-level
stream-of-consciousness technique in which reflection and
spontaneous feeling combine to produce a picture of the player
watching himself playing. Thus:

> As he ran about there seemed to be two parts of his
> brain. One followed the ball, deciding when to tackle
> and when to fall back. The other seemed to talk back to
> him, as though he was really two people, one making a
> speech to the other.
>
> *Go in hard. No time for fancy-work in juvenile football. Go
> in hard and don't waste time. One day play like Bobby Evans.
> Not really fond of playing wing-half. Centre-forward best
> position. Be Billy Houliston. Rummle 'em up.*
>
> *One thing you've got – iron determination. Hard as nails.
> Don't care about being hurt. Only get hurt if you go in half-
> hearted. Do or die.*

Dunky's aspirations in turning out for Cartneuk are broadly
romantic – he wants to emulate the Scottish footballers of the
day; he wants to impress the girls. However, this *Boy's Own Paper*
view of soccer is balanced by a matter-of-fact acceptance of the
spirit in which this kind of soccer gets played:

At school it was all sportsmanship. You didn't play to win, oh no, you were told off for fouling ... But once you were out in real football it was different. The ref could only give fouls against you, not treat you like a wee boy. And Baldy was only interested in playing to win. As long as you didn't give away penalties or get sent off, Baldy didn't care what you did.

Technically, this is not an enormous distance from another lost 1960s classic – B.S. Johnson's *The Untouchables* (1969). The subject matter of this experimental *cause célèbre* (its 27 sections came packed into a cardboard box and could be read in any order that the reader chose) occasionally takes second place to the aesthetic principles involved, but twisting among the laments for a dead friend named 'Tony' are some spirited stream-of-consciousness accounts of trying to report a football match for the *Observer*.

In the end Dunky's soccer career is overtaken by the spirit of fatalism with which the whole of *From Scenes Like These* is gradually infused. Promoted to Cartneuk's first team for a cup final, he overdoes the 'do or die' exhortations and winds up in hospital with a broken arm and two missing front teeth (kicked out by an enraged opponent). But all Dunky's romantic dreams are fading away. An idealistic relationship with a girl called Elsa ends unhappily. Drinking with his mates, the whole seductive baggage of 'being a man' seems suddenly preferable to playing soccer. His nerve has gone as well. The book ends with an extended description of a boozy Hogmanay celebration, done rather in the manner of Irvine Welsh but with alcohol taking the place of drugs.

It seems clear, from the intensity of these descriptions, that Williams had played the game himself. The same is certainly true of J.L. Carr's *How Steeple Sinderby Wanderers Won The FA Cup* (1975), whose detailed observation of soccer at the village level owes something to Carr's own career in local sides in the 1930s (bizarrely, just before his death in 1994 Carr reissued *Sinderby* under his own Quince Tree Press imprint – he was for many years a small publisher of immense distinction – styling it 'non-fiction' and including a photograph of 'The South Milton Team' for whom he had turned out 64 years before). Carr solves the problem of writing realistically about the realities of sport by pretending not to – painting the Sinderby team's inexorable progress to Wembley (their mentor is an exiled Hungarian academic with revolutionary coaching theories) in a glow of romance, while simultaneously stoking up an authentic atmosphere of half-time oranges, liniment and old LNER railway carriages doing service as changing rooms. *Sinderby*'s utterly original flavour – largely done by means of pastiche – is difficult to convey without quotation, but Joe Gidner's committee meeting minutes give a fair idea of Carr's comic style: 'Mr Slingsby (Capt.), reporting on *interim progress*, stated that his team had defeated Hackthorn Young Conservatives (away) 13-0, N. Baddesley Congs. Tennis & Football Club (home) 14-0, Bennington British Rail (away) 12-0 and Aston Villa (at Wolverhampton) 2-1.' Or there is his round-up of press reports of the first-round draw:

> Only a handful of Hartlepool supporters will bother to travel to the little Welsh market town . . .' *Mirror*
> 'Steeple, the tiny Yorkshire colliery village, is host to Hartlepool . . .' *Telegraph*
> 'Old Grandfer Fangfoss, trainer of the villagers, squeezed a chuckle from his toothless jaws as he sat over a noggin beside his cottage door. "Oi sez our lads'll win 'em, mi jollys," he piped, running a horny hand over his luscious sixteen-year-old bride's bouncy boobies . . .' *The Sun*

Inevitably, perhaps, *How Steeple Sinderby Wanderers Won The FA*

Cup is really a novel about loss – the book is presented as an interim report in advance of the official history compiled by the secretary after the final when the team has broken up. On the final page Mr Fangfoss, the megalomaniac chairman who bestrides the novel like a colossus, finds Gidner loitering in the market square. 'I know what you're looking for,' he gruffly consoles him. 'But it's all gone, and it'll never come back.'

Brian Glanville, B.S. Johnson, Gordon M. Williams, J.L. Carr: a list of great, or even halfway decent, soccer writers would barely exhaust the fingers of one hand. One recent arrival on the roster might be the Indian novelist Nalinaksha Bhattacharya, whose 1992 debut *Hem and Football* features a thirteen-year-old Calcutta schoolgirl named Hemprova ('Hem') Mintra. Hem's attempt to detach herself from the stifling bonds of family and social expectation is buttressed by selection for the Champaboti Girls' High School XI, and an eventual trial for the first Bengali professional club for women. Whimsically comic in its effects, as in the Marxist coach Miss Nag, who relates the principles of the *Communist Manifesto* to the team's performance ('the whole thing only makes sense if we consider ourselves as proletarians and our opponents as the bourgeoisie', Hem's friend Tanya explains) or the epigraph from Tommy Docherty's *Better Football*, Bhattacharya's novel actually covers some of the same territory as *Fever Pitch*. In each case soccer, at once refuge, palliative and escape route, ceases to be soccer and takes on a wholly figurative significance.

Given the game's ultra-fashionable status, one might expect literary London to be swarming with muscular young novelists keen to recast a great deal of on-field or touchline experience into fictional form: the semi-exploitative horrors of John King's soccer violence novel *The Football Factory* (1996) demonstrate that this trend is fairly well advanced. On the other hand a trawl through the 'serious' fiction of the last decade or so yields up only the dream sequence (in which a man imagines himself to be playing for Leicester City) in Julian Barnes' *A History of the World in 10½ Chapters* (1989); *Putting The Boot In* (1985), one of the 'Duffy' private investigator spoofs by Barnes' alter-ego Dan Kavanagh, also has a soccer background, and there are a few cursory, streetwise references in Martin Amis. It is an odd fact, but unquestionably true, that for most serious writers soccer is still an excuse for slightly bemused (or knowing, depending on the circumstances) condescension. Here, for instance, is Martin Amis appraising the Saturday afternoon maelstrom of Loftus Road in the voice of Keith Talent:

> 'They're away today,' said Keith through his cigarette. 'United, innit. I was there *last* week.'
>
> 'West Ham. Any good?'
>
> Some of the light went out in Keith's blue eyes as he said, 'During the first half the Hammers probed down the left flank. Revelling in the space, the speed of Sylvester Dragon was always going to pose problems for the home side's number two. With scant minutes remaining before the half-time whistle, the black winger cut in on the left back and delivered a searching cross converted by Lee Fredge . . .'

Jolly funny and all that – although Amis's tabloid jargon piss-take is about a decade out of date – but the passage (from *London Fields*, 1989) is not inserted to illustrate Martin Amis's interest in football; it exists as a vehicle to enable Amis to do what he does best – poke fun at the working classes. A much better idea of football's centrality to a certain kind of working-class world can be found in the off-centre dialogues of Gordon Legge's *In Between Talking About The Football*. To give you an idea of the habitual, lofty incomprehension that attends any attempt to mingle the near-hermetically sealed compartments of 'soccer' and 'the English novel', a couple of years back I took part in one of those 'Whither the novel?' colloquia. This took place, almost inevitably, at a bookshop in Hampstead. So, enquired one exasperated punter, at the end of a group disparagement of nearly every fancied modern writer, what should novelists be writing about? Well, I diffidently suggested, if novelists were going to write about 'ordinary life' – representations of which the audience seemed generally keen on – what about some brave spirit writing a book about a Premiership football side? 'Heaven forbid' shouted a malcontent in the back row amid whinnies of disagreement. On another occasion I produced a novel in which an American management consultant is despatched to take stock of a struggling lower division side named Walham Town and is compelled to sit – in a state of some bewilderment – through a couple of games. Among other things this produced a puzzled review in the *Times Literary Supplement* wondering whether a football crowd would really have chanted the words 'XYZ is a homosexual' in jocular abuse of one of the players, and, if so, how would the first 'o' be sounded? Delicious, isn't it? Football is a central experience to the upbringing of about half the UK's adult male population, but to take it seriously – even to suggest that it might have some enduring relevance for the creative writer – is seen as a kind of cultural slumming. There is, heaven knows, enough snobbery currently disfiguring the English novel, and it would be a pity if it discouraged closer attention to a game which, more than any other national sport, is crying out to have novels written about it.

fantasy finals

D . J .   T A Y L O R

Twenty miles along the M6 the minivan broke down. They stood in a semi-circle on the hard shoulder rubbing their hands together against the raw Pennine dawn, while Alex hobbled the 500 yards down the motorway to call the AA. Coming back from the emergency phone, hearing the surge of the oncoming traffic as it flew dangerously towards him, he saw them loitering stiffly in the pale early light, drinking tea out of flasks and swapping cigarettes. There were red and white scarves knotted over the back of the van, with a slogan that Alex hadn't seen until now – ALEX FERGUSON'S RED AND WHITE ARMY – sprayed in shaving foam on the rear windscreen. They were good lads, Alex thought. Hell, they were the best. Half an hour later, slamming the bonnet down into its frame, the AA patrolman noticed the scarves and the piled Umbro bags. 'Are you some kind of sports team?' he asked.

High up in the Hotel Pompadour, with its dizzying views out over the level Hertfordshire plain, the boys killed time: lingered by the shining surface of the 50-metre swimpool, drank half bottles of Bollinger in the Marie-Antoinette Lounge or strolled moodily through the lush pasturages of Axminster and polished pine. A handful – always that intent, stolid handful – kept to their suites and trained.

'OK. Words that sound the same but with different meanings. One: contraceptive and town in south-west France?'

'Condom.'

'*Check*. Two: baby's nappy and eighteenth-century poet?'

'A what?'

'Eighteenth-century poet is what it says here.'

'Diaper.'

Trevor smiled. 'Nice one Leroy. You want to me to try you on Chemistry? You were weak on that in the semis.'

'Go ahead.'

'A white crystalline dextrorotatory sugar found in the form of xylon in wood and straw?'

Leroy beamed in a smile made famous by a hundred fan-posters, souvenir programmes and TV docs. 'Xylose,' he mouthed happily. '*Xylose*.'

Ten miles south of Birmingham they stopped at a Happy Eater for coffee. Coming back from the phone again – if Doreen didn't return those library books this morning they'd get another sodding warning letter – Alex noticed that there was something wrong about the ellipse of hunched, muscular shoulders, the double row of bony, cropped heads that occasionally banged together as their owners bent over the narrow table, the better to apply themselves to the platefuls of chips and the monstrous, glistening doughnuts. What was wrong was that there were only ten of them.

'Where's Andy then?'

In the long, uneasy silence that followed only Gary was prepared to catch Alex's eye.

'He couldn't come boss.'

'Why couldn't he come?'

'Said he didn't feel like it . . . Besides, that Sharon – you heard they got married? – said he ought to go to the sales with her and her mum.'

'Christ! You know what this means?'

The faces hung and stared, fists halfway to swollen mouths, eyes popping over the formica. They knew he was a hard bastard, Alex reflected, but they respected him.

'It means,' he said, 'that I'll have to play myself.'

Supine on the leopardskin sunbed, mobile cradled in the nook formed by head and splayed elbow, Ken Fantoni listened to the poolside chatter.

'How much did you get for that interview with *Hello*?' Trevor demanded.

'Which interview?'

'The one about you and Greta Scacchi. The one where you reckoned she . . .'

'Oh, *that* interview . . . Ten.'

'Barry got fifteen for that piece about how he remembers stuff with mnemonics.'

'*Fifteen*!' Leroy shook his head sternly. 'I'm going to have to talk to Ron about this.'

'Wow,' Trevor breathed admiringly. 'You never told me your agent was *Ron*.'

Even now, Fantoni reflected, even now, four hours before the game, with a hundred thousand people on their way to the stadium, with security fighting off the tabloid reporters in the foyer, with the agents' phones burning white-hot with ever more outrageous demands for camcorders, round-the-world flights and virtual reality machines, it was hard to resist a certain complacency. The papers – *Quizmaster* and *Brainbox* – had been sceptical at first, but three months later here they were with the world at their feet. Inevitably, they'd had their share of the breaks. Buying Carlsson from Trondheim had been a lucky one, what with that question about Ibsen in the third round. And who'd have thought Wayne – Wayne of all people – would have memorised a complete list of the English county towns? Fantoni glanced at his watch: ten minutes until the Sky TV crew arrived. Ignoring the respectful nods from the boys, from Barry and Wayne and Trevor, staked out in all their boxer-shorted splendour, he lumbered off to the Louis Quatorze Suite, where only last week, the hotel had hastened to assure him, a Saudi prince and his retinue had been accommodated for the night.

Nosing their way eastward along the North Circular, caught up in the ebb and drift of the Cup final traffic, Alex listened to the voices from the back seats.

'Fucking good idea of someone's to pick the same day as the fucking Cup final.'

'Think the Red Lion'll win?'

'Stands to reason dunnit? He's unbelievable, that Carlsson. I saw him in the League against Thetford Dog and Ferret. Ten questions about Brookside and he got the fucking lot.'

'And he's fucking Norwegian as well. Makes you think.'

Even now, Alex reflected, even now, with a full-strength side – well, nearly a full-strength side, with Ryan let off his paper round for once – it was hard to believe that they weren't going to get steamrollered. Unexpectedly, they'd had their share of the breaks. Chelsea not turning up in the third had been a bonus, though. And who'd have guessed Roy's dad would have been owed a favour by the ref in the fifth? Alex glanced at his watch: ten minutes until the time he'd promised to phone Doreen again. Ignoring the V-signs from the boys and the glimpse of the two brothers, Phil and Gary, hunched over their tattered copy of *Gentleman's Relish*, he eased the van into the nearside lane and started looking for a phone box that took money rather than sodding phonecards.

'Naturally I'm very proud of the lads,' Fantoni told the reporter from BSkyB. 'I mean, I found Wayne making notes out of the

Bloomsbury Guide To English Literature the other day at training: I don't think you can ask for much more commitment than that...Terry? Now don't get me wrong, Tel's done a great job with the Trowel and Hammer lads – the way they came back against the King's Head in the semis was brilliant – but I think there has to be a question mark over their in-depth knowledge. Politics. TV and Leisure. Entomology. These are all areas where we'll be looking for an early advantage. Of course, I'd have paid two million for Darren Guscott if I'd had the chance, but you've got to remember the lad's only nineteen and he's never going to get those '70s pop questions is he?'

'Fingers crossed, love,' Alex told his wife. 'This is the big one.'

In the hush of the Wembley tunnel, a minute before they stepped out into the bright, coruscating glare, Fantoni stole a look at his team – Wayne taking a last-second glance at his pocket edition of *Who's Who in Showbiz*, Leroy and Barry pooling information on Danish coastal resorts, the subs, Darryl and Maurice, nervously combing their hair in hand-mirrors. Hearing the boom of the taped music, pumped from a hundred speakers high above the concrete – they were playing 'The March of the Gladiators' – Fantoni thought he was going to cry. He remembered his early days, crouched in the corner of a sweaty pub in Shoeburyness while his dad, old Frank Fantoni, failed to answer questions on pre-war film actresses, his humble apprenticeship as unpaid coach to a non-league winebar in Macclesfield. And now this! Somewhere in the distance a bell rang. Staring resolutely in front of him, Fantoni strode out to meet the wall of dense and noiseless sound.

When they got to the ground, a bare, grassless rectangle flanked on both sides by teams of girls playing six-a-side hockey, the

West Ham team were already warming up. A dozen spectators smoked cigarettes or bickered cheerlessly. Alex, regarding them gloomily, noted that they were big lads all right and hoped things wouldn't get out of hand. For a second he felt a brief pang of nostalgia for his old hobby, but the local Boys' Brigade branch had closed now and they hadn't wanted him as a Scoutmaster. Trudging across from the changing room, the reek of disinfectant still hanging in the air, he watched Eric point disparagingly at the pitch. *'Merde!'* he said – somehow Alex could never get over the fact that Eric was French – 'They might at least have shifted the dog turds.'

In the end it all went the way Fantoni had predicted. Before the cameras' dense, vaporous stare, beneath the urgent baying of the crowd, the Red Lion took an early lead through Carlsson's knowledge of the Hanseatic timber trade and lost it again when Leroy failed to define the word 'paronomasia'. With one question to go the Trowel and Hammer were a point behind. As Guscott stepped up to the dais, his pale teenager's face twisted with tension, the crowd fell silent.

'Which group in the early 1970s had three singles which entered the charts at Number One?'

Guscott whinnied slightly, gazed in anguish from right to left, guessed wildly: 'Abba?'

Amid a mounting crescendo of noise the tuxedo'd MC shook his head. 'Sorry son. The correct answer is Slade.'

'Lost six-nil,' Alex informed Doreen. 'No, they were big lads. Eric and Paul got sent off for fighting . . . They're keeping Nicky in overnight for observation.' Outside rain fell over the grey London streets. 'Eleven o'clock then, but I promised Roy I'd drop him off at the station, and you know Ryan's mum doesn't like him staying out late.'

★ ★ ★

In the hospitality suite Fantoni graciously accepted his fifth daiquiri and tried to concentrate on what the interviewer was saying.

'So what about Europe, Ken? Do you think you can repeat this success on the international stage?'

Fantoni yawned. He was thinking of changing his girlfriend. Mitzi was OK but you couldn't take her to the European Cup final could you? What about that girl who read the ITV weather? He'd ask Ron about it.

'Ken?'

'Definitely Alan. Munich Bierkeller. Estaminet Georges Pompidou Marseilles. I know they play a different style over there – Economics, Art and Literature, they have university professors turning pro these days – but I'm confident we can beat these Continentals at their own game . . .'

'Fantasy Finals' appears in D.J. Taylor's forthcoming collection of short stories, After Bathing at Baxter's *(Vintage, £5.99).*

i believe your son's cocked it up, old girl

JORGE VALDANO

Juan Antonio Felpa was a placid man, but he decided to ensure a good night's sleep before the day of the match by taking a sleeping pill, for he was anxious, and not without reason. He woke as usual at seven in the morning and the butterflies in his stomach immediately told him that it was Sunday, football day, so he decided to stay in bed a bit longer to think about the match. He spent several minutes saving penalties in identical fashion. It was his favourite dream, his recurring fantasy: 0-0 with a minute to go and a penalty against; expectant hush, wide-eyed onlookers, the correct hunch and himself in the air with his arms around the ball; or sometimes on the ground, fully deserving the applause, responsible for the flutter of emotion in the hundreds of fans; 0-0 the final score. Sometimes he imagined the same thing with his team winning 1-0, but he was less keen on this version, because it meant sharing the glory with the teammate who scored the goal. Juan Antonio Felpa, a worker at Fábricas Unidas and goalkeeper of the Atlético Sports Club, had a silly smile on his face when he mentally stopped penalties, although he did not know this.

He considered the weather as anxiously as any farmer; he leaped out of bed and made for the door, praying that it wasn't raining. On that 16 September of 1964, spring had beaten the calendar by five days. It was a perfect morning. The sun that filled him with life reminded him of his father's illness. 'A Peron day', his father would have said. He would go and visit him soon, to help the old man forget for a while his sadness at missing the classic.

He went into the modern kitchen for a cup of tea, as was his custom on Sundays, but could not get the match out of his head. He fixed his eyes on a crumpled poster of Amadeo Carrizo that he had stuck on the wall years before. Without ever having seen them play he had always been a supporter of River Plate. Buenos Aires was many miles away and a different kind of place, but through the radio and the magazine *El Grafico* he idealised the path of the team from the capital, and of its legendary goalkeeper. Since to admire a man is to identify with him, Felpa felt he was the Carrizo of the little town. He had copied some of his gestures and had even got hold of a chequered cap like the one the River Plate goalkeeper used to protect him from the sun. 'Maestro,' Juan Antonio murmured at the photograph of Amadeo, just as his wife came into the kitchen, heavy-eyed with sleep.

'Talking to yourself.'

'No, thinking.'

He accepted Mercedes' tender young kiss and they chatted for quite a long while about their own uncomplicated affairs.

They both listened to Johnny Lombard announcing the match. 'At five o'clock this evening at Las Parejas, the ground shared by Sportivo and Argentino, the league title will be decided in the most eagerly awaited match of the year.' The emotive voice, transported slowly in a car and amplified by two large loudspeakers on the roof, succeeded in making Felpa feel important. He broke into goose pimples.

There were still five matches to go to the end of the championship and the two teams – the blues of Argentino and the green-and-reds of Sportivo – shared first place in the Cañada Football League. This evening, honour and disgrace would be at stake, deciding once and for all who was who in the league.

For a week now people had talked of nothing else. Bets had been laid, jokes had come thick and fast, and the more impatient had already had the occasional punch-up. There was no mistaking from the atmosphere that the match was to be the most important classic of recent times.

'How are things in the factory?' asked Mercedes.

'Well . . . you know . . . the boys have driven me mad this week.'

Juan Antonio told his wife proudly that the boss had slapped him on the back and said, 'Juan, you'd better be good on Sunday, eh?'

Felpa was a decent fellow, 26 years old, not long married and with a baby a few months old. He had simple tastes, was generally well liked, and was the type of man who, while not having much, did not hanker for more. He dressed in his Sunday clothes, checked his sports bag, peeped fondly and noiselessly into his sleeping son's room, and said an unceremonious goodbye to his wife.

In the San Luis sanatorium, sitting on the bed where his father was convalescing from a stomach operation, he patiently accepted advice on football. They remembered the day they had gone hunting and Juan Antonio, aged ten, had run out and flung himself face down on a hare his father was trying to shoot with his old shotgun. The hare had got away and this rash attempt at goalkeeping – hurling himself upon any random object – was rewarded with a thrashing he would never forget. That was when they began calling him Cat. His father, a strong character who loved Sportivo as ardently as he hated Argentino, had never agreed with his son being a keeper, and not only because he frightened the hares. He had always thought that goalkeepers were halfwits. But he loved his only son so much that he cast his prejudice aside and ended up watching the games from behind the goal, although his shouts irritated more than they encouraged.

In his hospital bed, Don Jesús Eladio Felpa was feeling better, but not being able to watch the classic made him very agitated. He would have to resign himself to opening the windows of his room so as to interpret the cries reaching him from the pitch. At a distance of 200 metres, he would be able, by straining his ears, to identify dangerous attacks, decide which team was on top, and probably to attribute the goals scored to the correct team. Thirty-five years of going to Sportivo had taught him much. His poor wife had had to suffer in silence the rough and ready account Don Jesús gave of the games. Juan Antonio walked to the stadium, taking with him a last piece of fatherly advice: 'Save five goals, so they'll never talk again.'

On the way, he again began creating a penalty in his head. He always threw himself to the right and caught a moderately high shot. 'Hope is a waking dream,' he had once heard someone say.

At the ground he saw more people than ever before and an atmosphere of impending war. Hands alighted on his shoulders like uncouth butterflies, and he replied with a smile to the same old comments: 'Don't worry, they won't even get close today . . .' 'At five the shutters will come down, eh?' 'Who could this lot beat . . .?' He reached the calm of the restaurant and greeted his teammates, most of them from nearby villages and towns. He had not seen them since last Sunday. Most of them were good sorts, but he envied Argentino its ability to attract players from the town. 'Iti' Perazzo had a good explanation: 'People from the town play for the team colours; the outsiders play for the money.' But it had always been that way, and in all truth there was not much money at Sportivo.

They ate roast meat and salad, and afterwards 'Spooky' Mirage, an ex-player and at this particular moment the coach, told them the line-up and uttered the usual rubbish with the air of a man who had invented football.

The Felpas, father and son, could not stand Mirage because he had never cared for local football. The further away the team took him, the happier he was. What was more, he played without 'wingers' and made lots of tactical errors. The two were of one mind about the day 'Negro' Moyano had hailed Mirage in the middle of the Victoria bar.

'How goes it, Clutch?'

'Why, Clutch?' the coach had asked incautiously.

'Because first you step on the gas, and afterwards you change gears,' 'Negro' had said, making everybody laugh.

The players decided to travel to the pitch in four cars that belonged to members of the club's board. They left the restaurant by the back door so as not to give an opportunity to any loudmouths. In the changing room they began breathing the air of a match. It smelled of football here. The game was approaching and outside the noise was growing. With nerves taut they dressed, massaged themselves, and went through the warm-up as if it were some kind of religious ritual.

'The Cat' Felpa, in his corner, moved only his arms. Occasionally he would punch the air like a boxer. He put on his knee protectors and the shorts that were padded at the hips to deaden the impact of falls. He did not use gloves, and did not understand how you could save with them. When anyone asked him, he had learned a phrase that he enjoyed repeating: 'They rob me of sensitivity.' The tools he worked with during the week had made his hands strong, and he liked to feel the ball between his fingers.

As was their custom, the team formed a circle, piled their hands on top of the captain's and uttered three war cries. It gave them confidence and made them feel more united. It also served to scare the players in the next changing room.

They went through the tunnel to the music of leather boots

hitting the ground, and took care not to slip on the concrete. When they emerged, the red-and-green half of the stadium erupted. The blues were occupying the opposite stand and honoured their players three minutes later. The whole town was there.

It was a great day, one that was talked about in town for weeks: flags, ticker tape, drums, giant rattles; nothing was missing.

The referee's lecture was brief. 'Play and don't talk,' he told the captains in the centre circle before he tossed for ends.

The roar of the crowd and the emotions stirred by what was at stake lent some dignity to the poor football played in the first half. The two teams were trying to exploit any slackness in their opponents, but without weakening their own defences. They were afraid of each other and tense, and that resulted in a laboured and unfocused match.

Don Jesús Eladio Felpa, summing up the first half to his wife in the sanatorium, hit the nail on the head. 'Poor match, old girl. They are not creating chances.' They were certainly playing badly, but they were playing seriously. The legs were working hard and harsh words were heard between the players.

The second half seemed a bit more open, but neither team got into the penalty box much. Both sides wasted some chances, but these were the outcome not of passes but of lucky bounces or of mistakes made by tired legs.

But no one leaves a local derby before time. Again Don Jesús accurately informed his wife with some 15 minutes to go that 'something might still happen'. In this second half, Juan Antonio had donned his cap because the sun was low and shining in his face. His few interventions had been carried out soberly, except for the curving shot that he had cleared over the bar, diving backwards, a save that was more spectacular than difficult. From his goal he gave orders, encouraged his team-mates, and never lost concentration for a moment. Until the point in the game that no one who was there would ever forget, the match had not given him a chance to make a fool of himself.

Four minutes to go to the final whistle when 'Gringo' Santoni, always in such a hurry, unnecessarily gave away a corner. The time had come when the less interested were looking at their watches, willing it to be over at last; only the drunks were talking, and the fanatics had clambered onto the barriers, completely disenchanted. The corner was coming hard and 'The Cat' Felpa, it must be admitted, hesitated over coming out and stayed halfway. Antŭna, 'The Bear', Argentino's central defender, had no need to jump to head the ball smack against the angle of bar and post. 'Tiny' Zarate, who because of his height could not mark anybody tall and who was charged at corners with guarding the front post, knew instinctively that he could never reach the ball with his head. He cleared it with a slap of the hand. Penalty!

That roused the indifferent spectators, froze the fanatics and silenced the drunks. The blue side of the stadium started celebrating and the Sportivo crowd waited, motionless and speechless, for the gods of football to lend them a hand. It was turning out very much like Juan Antonio Felpa's fantasy.

At the other side of the pitch the sun had sunk behind the cypresses and Felpa, standing in the middle of the goal-line, took off his cap, very resolutely, and threw it into the goal. He felt a pleasant coolness on his sweating head, and perhaps that is why he experienced the faith of heroes.

Twelve yards away, 'Beto' Nieva was already standing behind the ball. They exchanged a fleeting glance, half accomplice and half assassin.

Juan Antonio Felpa flexed his knees slightly, and with his eyes fixed on the striker he listened to the referee's orders. He had already made up his mind. When 'Beto' struck the ball, Felpa was already flying in the direction of his dream. Beside the right-hand post he caught the ball in the air and before he hit the ground he felt, like a flash of lightning, the greatest joy of his life.

Now it was the red-and-green half of the ground that had started to celebrate, yelling 'Felpa', 'Fel-pa', 'Fel-pa'.

I do not know myself what happened in that moment, because in 25 years nobody has managed to talk to Felpa about it without angering him. But as I see it, the shouts confused him and caused him to embark on the most ridiculous course of his life. The fact is that he arose from the ground on a high, and, in an attempt to prolong the magic moment, made the mistake of going to fetch his cap from inside the goal with the ball under his arm. The referee hesitated before giving the goal, and everyone in the stadium slowly put their hands to their heads amid euphoric blue laughter and flabbergasted groans from the red-and-greens. The strange chorus of mutterings that continued to hang in the air baffled Don Jesús Eladio Felpa, who had suffered over the penalty ('But you have to admit it was fair, old girl') and had rejoiced over the fantastic save. He knew intuitively that something bad had happened. With a faint hope that he was mistaken, he looked at his saintly wife and remarked in a voice somewhere between sadness and concern: 'I believe your son's cocked it up, old girl.'

Translated by Mary Turton.

only sixty-four years

DANNIE ABSE

In the authorised silence of the house, upstairs in my bedroom, long past the fidgety tick of midnight, I lie horizontal under the sheets, my head on the pillow. The curtains are drawn. My wife, inert, asleep beside me. I stare at the back of my eyelids. This is the Waiting Room of Sleep. Before I am called to the other side of the adjoining door's frosted window something needs to inhabit the restless mind.

I confess that during those last wakeful moments which stretch and elongate with advancing age like shadows moving away from a night lamppost, I frequently summon eleven blue-shirted Cardiff City football players, along with three substitutes, into the now crowded Waiting Room to autograph Sleep's Visitors' Book. I have done so intermittently over many decades. Different players file in, one by one. All wear the Bluebird shirt. Some announce their famous names: Trevor Ford, John Charles, Mel Charles, Ivor Allchurch, all of whom played for Cardiff City in their declining football years.

What a pathetic confession! What a ridiculous obsession! Am I a baby needing a sort of dummy before I can fall asleep?

Here I am, a grown-up man, indeed an old man, still dreamily involved with a relatively down-and-out Division Three soccer team. More than that, I'm hungry for Cardiff City news: who's asked for a transfer? who's injured? who's in, who's out? what happened to X and will Ryan Giggs really sign for Cardiff?

In recent years I have become friendly with Leslie Hamilton, the Cardiff City doctor. Sometimes, when the Bluebirds play in or near London where I spend three-quarters of my life, he invites me to join him in the directors' box and enjoy the backstage pre-match and half-time hospitality of the home side. Always first, though, a sighing admonition: 'You can't come like that, Dannie. You have to be suitably dressed.' The short-haired businessmen who populate the boardrooms of football are stuffily rank conscious. Some Saturdays I wear a tie.

I must irritate my friend, Dr Hamilton, not only sartorially. Because I want to hear the latest Cardiff City gossip, the behind-the-scenes misdoings and machinations, the comings and goings, the resignations and aspirations, the betrayals of the last manager, the style of the new one, I sometimes clutch Dr Hamilton's lapels and cross-examine him. He, alas, remains, as a doctor should, invincibly discreet. Or I display my own swanking medical knowledge and query the constituents of the team's pre-match diet or propose, 'Given the absence of joint changes on clinical and X-ray examination; given normal laboratory findings, maybe it's just a psychogenic arthralgia?' How often he diverts my penetrative suggestions or diagnoses by telling me that he met someone who writes poetry. 'One of the players?' I ask hopefully, remembering the forgettable verses of ex-Cardiff City centre-forward, John Toshack.

I learn more about happenings at Ninian Park by reading the *South Wales Football Echo* which I have sent to me at my London home all season. Even when I worked as Writer-in-Residence at Princeton University, New Jersey 08540, USA for the 1973–74 academic year, I ensured that the pink newspaper regularly reached our rented home in Pine Street. I did not subscribe to the *Times Literary Supplement*, the *New Statesman*, the *Listener*, or the *Spectator*. I needed to keep in touch only with vital news.

More important, of course, than football chatter is watching the actual games. This I did and this I do for I am a season-ticket holder. I arrange my frequent sojourns in South Wales to coincide with Cardiff's home fixtures. If invited to give a poetry reading at Hereford or Hartlepool or Scunthorpe or any other sad Division Three town I scan the Bluebirds' fixture list to suggest a particular Saturday evening date so that I can be rewarded by watching my team play on that same away-day afternoon.

Once upon a youthful time I often shared a platform or stage at a provincial town hall, theatre, library or pub, with Laurie Lee. When we were offered a tandem gig somewhere in the United Kingdom it used to worry me that Laurie would consult his address book to see if he had a friend, for all I know a girl friend, in this or that town whereas I merely fumbled yet again for the City fixture list. Dummy. Dummy. Cider only with the Bluebirds and not a Rosie in sight. Were, and are, my priorities wrong?

'If you want to go, you're on your own,' insisted my seventeen-year-old brother, Leo.

'The *Echo* reckons they'll do better than last season,' I said, trying to persuade my big brother to take me to Ninian Park.

'They couldn't do worse.'

'They've eight new players,' I mumbled.

Almost a year earlier I had seen my first game. Leo had allowed me to accompany him to watch the Bluebirds play Torquay United. We had joined 18,000 jugular critics for that Division Three (South) match. City had lost only 0–1, so I was hooked!

That 1933–34 season when I first became a fan, Cardiff City's ponderous and awkward defence leaked 105 goals. If they, surprisingly, scored first then the headlines in the *South Wales*

Echo would inevitably read BLUEBIRDS FLATTER TO DECEIVE. They finished bottom of Division Three and, pleadingly, had to seek re-election – their worst season in their history. Only a few years earlier, in the previous decade, the Bluebirds had been Division One League Championship runners-up, FA Cup finalists and FA Cup winners. But since 1929 they'd slid down the league tables as if greased. How are the mighty fallen! Tell it not at the Kop, publish it not in the streets of Highbury, lest the daughters of Swansea Town rejoice.

Though I had never seen them in their prime, they were still my heroes. When I kicked a football in Roath Park or a tennis ball in the back lane with villain Phillip Griffiths, I underwent a wondrous metamorphosis. I wore an invisible royal blue shirt and I responded to the name of speedy Reg Keating, the City centre-forward, a blur of blue, who was known to have once scored a goal. So I was very disappointed that on Saturday, 25 August 1934, Leo would not take me to Ninian Park because, as he said, they lost all the time.

So what? We always seemed to back losers in our house. We sided with the workers but the capitalists continued to water the workers' beer. Hadn't he, himself, taught me an alternative rhyming alphabet which began – A stands for Armaments, the capitalist's pride, B stands for Bolshie, the thorn in their side? We voted Labour, didn't we? But around our patch they always lost the elections. Leo drummed into me that the Red Indians were the good guys not the imperialist cowboys. It was true too: Saturday mornings at the Globe cinema, the cowboys, led by Tom Mix, always won. And hadn't I heard my mother muttering, shaking her head, 'Your Dad's a loser.' Was she, I wonder, only talking about horses and greyhounds?

It was my gentle and beloved father, though, who one Saturday of late August sunlight financed me – pennies for the tramcar journey, sixpence for the game – so that I could go ON

MY OWN, for the first time, to Ninian Park. Still only ten years high, I set out on this daring expedition from our semi-detached house in Albany Road. I don't remember my farewell in the hallway but I bet my mother fussed and kissed me goodbye as if I were going on a trek to the North Pole.

An hour or so later I stood outside the Ninian Park stadium disconsolate. I searched through my pockets once more only to find the used tram ticket, pennies for my return journey and the handkerchief that my mother had pushed into my pocket before I left the house. The sixpence had vanished, the little silver sixpenny bit, so generously given to me despite business being so bad and Australia winning the final Test match by 562 runs, had become invisible.

All around me people fined through the turnstiles. Someone was shouting, 'Programmes, getcher programme,' and another fellow with a strange Schnozzle Durante croak attempted to sell the converging crowds this or that differently coloured rosette. There were policemen on foot and policemen on horses and amid all the whirl of movement a few stood lazily in front of an unhygienic-looking van whose owner in a white coat purveyed sizzling sausages and onions.

I listened glumly to the conversations of those standing at the van. I don't recall what they were saying. Perhaps they spoke fondly of the old days, of the great players who wore the royal blue shirt – Fred Keanor, Hardy, Ferguson and Farquharson, legendary figures before my time. I did not know what they were saying and soon, in any case, they moved off. No one loitered near the sausage van. Gradually the crowds in Sloper Road thinned out, to join the flat-capped masses swaying in the swearing terraces. I could hear the military band playing within the ground. I stood there, close to tears, knowing the misery of the world and that Outside is a lonely place.

How did I lose that sixpence? On the way maybe, upstairs

in the smoke-filled tram? Had I pulled the handkerchief out of my pocket and inadvertently sent the sixpenny bit rolling beneath one of the varnished wooden seats? Surely the pipe-smoking pensioner sitting next to me wasn't an evil, clever pickpocket? What would I tell them all when I returned home? Mama, I sat next to Bill Sikes.

A sudden, barbaric roar from the crowd within the stadium signalled that the teams had appeared from the tunnel. The game would soon begin. Still some stragglers hurried towards the turnstiles as I waited there, unwilling to retrace my steps down Sloper Road. Soon there were no longer any late-comers. I stood in solitary vigil listening to the crowd's oohs and resonant aahs, coming and fading now that the game had begun. I must have been crying for suddenly a gruff voice said, 'Whassermara, sonny?' He bent down, he was a police-man so he sided with the oppressors of the workers – Leo had told me. But when I confessed that I had lost my sixpence he advised, 'They let the unemployed in near the end of the game. They open the gates at the Grangetown end. You could slip in then, sonny.' He began to walk away. Then he changed his mind. He came back and gave me sixpence.

I joined the 20,000 spectators in Ninian Park who attended the first Division Three (South) game of the 1934–35 season. In the crowded Grangetown area between the goalposts I, umbilicus-high, tried to struggle through the massed supporters so that I could see my heroes. Suddenly, as was the custom with small boys, I was elevated by benign hands and passed down good-naturedly over capped heads to join other pygmies near the front. We beat Charlton Athletic 2–1 and Keating scored one of the goals. I thought you'd like to know that. Though we won those late summer matches we ended that season 19th in the league. As so often City 'flattered only to deceive'.

★ ★ ★

I am trying to recall in more detail how it used to be at Ninian Park before and after the old wooden Grand Stand, one evening in 1937, lit up with incandescent fury as it burned on and on and to the ground. The Canton Stand had not then been surgically abbreviated to render it safe to sit in. The Grangetown end, now open to the frequently raining Welsh skies, used to be steeper and higher and owned a long oblique roof. The Division Three crowds averaged 20,000 not the current 3,000.

Before the match a brass band, a uniformed platoon, would march around the touchlines, hoompa hoompa, as they played rhythmic military airs. Bollocks. And the same to you. Bollocks. A man pregnant with a huge drum would trail behind the platoon, while leading them an ostentatious conjurer would, at intervals, throw a somersaulting pole high into the air before catching it in his croupier-white gloves. How the crowd would have loved to observe that Clever Dick lose and drop it.

Just before kick-off the brass band would assemble outside the players' tunnel. When the team spurted on to the turf the band would strike up Cardiff's inappropriate, inanely optimistic, signature tune: HAPPY DAYS ARE HERE AGAIN. The crowd's welcoming shout to the emerging players would zenith to such decibels that the pigeons which, at one time, thrived under the roofs of the stands would fountain up and out and away.

In those sepia days before the war, season after season I, alone or with school friends, used to observe this pre-match ritual from behind the goalposts at the Grangetown end. Opposite, the length of the green pitch away, loomed the slanting roof of the Canton Stand on which was painted an advertisement for Franklyn's Tobacco. Beneath it, in the depths of the posterior darkness, small sparks of light would transiently appear here and there, above and below, to the left and to the right – evidence that the advertisement had been effective for the spectators were lighting up their pipes or cigarettes.

Before the commencement of the game, a flotilla of motorised wheelchairs carrying cripples of the first world war would settle below the wings of the Grand Stand behind the touchlines near the corner flags. By 1939 these odd, closed, ugly vehicles had become scarce but after the second world war, out of the smoke as it were, in an unhappy reincarnation, new wheelchair vehicles appeared. Years passed before they vanished from the scene.

So often have I visited Ninian Park in fine, wet, or wind-blown weather, have stood on the terraces, sat in the stands, been comfortable or bloody cold as I observed football fashions changing: the prolegomenon and the tactics on the pitch. Every-thing so different and so much the same. I see the brown ball become white, see it passed back to the goalkeeper who picks it up, though directed from his own teammate. I hear a referee's long whistle blow from a bygone year. How does the song go? I remember it well. And 1952 was a very good year: City returned (briefly, alas) to Division One and over 50,000 attended the final Second Division game against Leeds.

> Memory of faded games, the discarded years,
> talk of Aston Villa, Orient, and the Swans.
> Half-time, the band played the same military airs
> as when the Bluebirds once were champions.
> Round touchlines the same cripples in their chairs.

In those lean, utility, post-war years, before the introduction of floodlighting, fixtures began at 2.30 p.m. and the kick-off was even earlier mid-winter. Often, late in the game, the players in the smoke-brown, thickening gloom, would become, at the distant Canton end, anonymous astigmatic figures drifting this way or that without evident purpose. At the confusion of the final whistle, whatever the score – win, lose or draw – hordes of youngsters would invade the pitch. Some would bring on a ball

and incompetently kick it into the empty Grangetown end goal
with amazing delight, others would seek the players' autographs.
They were hardly chased off. They had become part of the
Saturday afternoon ritual.

Nor did one experience feelings of incipient threat as the
crowds dispersed into and through the dusk of Sloper Road.
Because money was scarcer, trains slower, motorways not yet
built, away fans did not usually attend the game in numbers. The
home crowd, being more homogeneous, shared the same gods
(who failed them), chanted the same chorus. They belonged to
the same defeated tribe.

Like many of the youngsters near the barrier behind the
goalposts I held back at the end of the match in order to avoid
the crush of the crowds converging through the big gates of
the Grangetown end. How quickly Ninian Park became empty,
forlorn, abandoned, as the unaccompanied small boys patiently
waited there. Outside the lampposts jerked into luminous
activity and somehow emphasised the oncoming darkness of a
December night.

How many occasions did I see City lose; how often the
thin, damp, Welsh rain descended in melancholy sympathy at
lighting-up time as I quit the ground into Sloper Road to
progress under the hoardings, to re-enter real life. 'South
Wales Echo, sir. Last edition. NAZIS ENTER RHINELAND.
Echo. Echo. Echo.'

Silent the stadium. The crowds have all filed out.
Only the pigeons beneath the roofs remain.
The clean programmes are trampled underfoot
and natural the dark, appropriate the rain
while under lampposts threatening newsboys shout.

In 1944, most weekdays, you could have found me in the

precincts of King's College in the Strand, more often than not on its fifth floor in the long Dissecting Room where, on slabs, anonymous dead human beings awaited medical students' scalpels. I cannot say I enjoyed studying the anatomy of the human body. Like other students I laid bare muscles, tendons, arteries and nerves until tissue-sections resembled the coloured plates in the anatomy text-book. At night, we had to take turns firewatching on the roof of King's College. It was not always unfathomably dark. Sometimes the moon transformed the fluent Thames below into a long, twisting slug of mercury; or long searchlight beams probed the arena of the sky; sometimes, too, the chug chug of a doodlebug, a pilotless rocket, alarmed the fire-watchers below. So it was a relief to escape into the calm of a Saturday afternoon and *play* football.

In *A Poet in the Family* I confessed how much I enjoyed those afternoons: 'I gained pleasure from playing rugby or cricket or tennis or squash – but soccer was something else. That season 1943–44, when I played for King's first eleven along with those other medical students, I enjoyed my soccer more than ever before. I can remember the details of some games with disturbing clarity. I am sure it sounds kinky, and I have never thought of myself as kinky, but I enjoyed my soccer then, at least on some days, as much as I have sexual intercourse on some nights with the right person.'

A few of the King's College team were chosen to represent London University. That was how I met Wyn Griffiths, a veterinary student based in Reading, a goalkeeper who also played for Cardiff City. (Later, after the war, he had games for Arsenal and indeed played in that smog-dense famous fixture against the Moscow Dynamos.) Just before Easter, after a London University match, Wyn Griffiths suggested I trained, during the holiday break, with the City team. 'Cyril Spiers, the manager, welcomes guest players,' Wyn told me.

So that springtime, excited, I ran too slowly over the green holy grass of Ninian Park and tried to pass the ball to players I admired, among them the winger, Beriah Moore, and the future Welsh international, Alf Sherwood. Afterwards, Cyril Spiers asked me if, the following Saturday, I should like to play for the Reserves in the Welsh League home match against Oswestry.

I returned to our house in Cathedral Road my chest stuck out for medals. Because my elder brothers, Wilfred and Leo, one in the Army, the other in the RAF, had both been posted abroad I could not boast to them. So, casually, I informed my father that I would be turning out for Cardiff City Reserves. 'Christ, they must be bloody short of players,' he opined. My mother, though, consoled me: 'Never mind, son, not everybody can play for the first team.'

That Saturday afternoon I did not wear the blue shirt of Cardiff City Reserves. Cyril Spiers took me aside in the dressing room and explained that only ten of the Oswestry team had turned up. 'Would you,' he continued politely, 'be good enough to play for them?' Oswestry? What could I say? I had never been to fatuous Oswestry, didn't want to go there either, though I knew they had a renowned orthopaedic centre and, come to think of it, wasn't it the place where Wilfred Owen was born? But I wanted to play for Cardiff not Oswestry.

Soon I was in the visitors' dressing room pulling over my head the red shirt of Oswestry Town and minutes later following strangers in other red shirts as we ambled on to the pitch. How daunting the deserted terraces and the emptiness of the stadium: 50 people, not 50,000, were about to observe my inept display.

What I remember best about the game is an incident half way through the second half. Minutes beforehand, I had experienced a cramp in my calf muscle so, instead of falling back into our own half, I doodled upfield in the centre-forward position. When the Oswestry right full back blasted an oblique long ball in a high trajectory to my left, I found myself clear and I was able to steer the ball towards the penalty area.

Here I was, this was no day dream. Good God, this was Ninian Park. The game so far had been goalless. I could be a hero. The goalposts were advancing towards me and I was being chased by some fast bugger in a blue shirt. In my dreams I would smash the ball high into the net beating the goalkeeper, as the *Football Echo* would put it, 'all ends up'. Fifty thousand frenetic supporters would scream, 'Goal.' My mouth tasted, 'Hallelujah.'

It did not turn out like that. I wore a red shirt, not a blue one. I heard not the voice of multitudes but the clear solitary cry of Cyril Spiers from the touchline: 'Now's your chance, son.'

The goalposts continued to advance towards me. At my heels the Cardiff City player was becoming intimate. The Cardiff City goalkeeper was leaving his area as if to welcome me. He narrowed the angle and the goalposts shrank to hockey size. 'Now's your chance, son.' A cry hanging in the air. I had not time to switch the ball from my left foot to my more certain right. I was running too fast. Surely I would be tripped up by the pagan, burly cipher behind me? But now I was in the penalty area and the undeceived goalkeeper, half crouching, still advanced. '. . . chance, son.' I prodded at the ball with my left foot as, almost simultaneously, I crashed into the green-jerseyed keeper. I saw the ball slither across the pigmented green turf and scrape the wrong side of the far talcum-white goalpost. The Grange-town Stand behind and above the crossbar yawned darkness and silence.

The goalkeeper, winded, soon revived, but I discovered that the patella of my right knee had been displaced upwards. It did not hurt, but after I'd pushed it down into its normal position I limped for the rest of the game. I merely loitered, in those days of no substitutes, more or less one-legged on the right wing until the final whistle blew.

I did not tell my father that I had played for Oswestry Town. Nor anybody else. My secret; even when my Uncle Sol, obviously briefed by my Dad, asked me how I got on playing for Cardiff City Reserves.

Often, when I sit in Block D, row M, of the Grand Stand at Ninian Park my eyes stray towards the Grangetown end goal-posts. Or rather, to the left upright. To be exact, to the foot of the left upright where an invisible X marks the spot where a ghost ball once scraped its outer side.

Decades ago, for one whole winter, I did not watch Cardiff City. A friend of mine, having been offered a temporary university teaching job in Connecticut, lent me his Grand Stand season ticket for the Spurs. The football proved to be much more classy, of course, than the scrappy long ball, adrenalin kick-about evident at Ninian Park. Some of the spectators were classy too. I sat next to Lewis Greifer, an old friend, script editor of the television series *Love Story*, and peered over the tidy parting of philosopher Freddie Ayer and the non-existent one of music critic Hans Keller. Behind me, though, camped a more conventional soccer fan who, on several occasions, brought with him a pre-puberty, diminutive boy who used to call out in his high pre-puberty voice to Cliff Jones or Danny Blanchflower, 'Well done, my son.'

The man himself, like the boy, all through the match sucked boiled sweets and every time Spurs scored I had to extract a sticky lump of orange, or raspberry, or lemon-coloured carbo-hydrate from the back of my neck. If I had shut my eyes for ninety minutes I could have known how many goals Tottenham had scored simply by counting the half-sucked acid drops that had unerringly landed above my collar. That could hardly happen at Ninian Park, where our forwards usually suffered from a goal famine.

The game that progressed below might have been a dramatic, mobile, altering diagram of subtlety and excellence, of Glory, Glory, Nice One Cyril and Hallelujah, but I did not feel partisan as I did and do when watching the Bluebirds' rare skills and common errors at Ninian Park. Academic appreciation is not enough. Visceral engagement spices even a bland routine game.

After that one-season betrayal in following a Rolls-Royce London team I invested, for the first time, in a Cardiff City Grand Stand season ticket. That year, I think it was 1963, the Bluebirds had been promoted temporarily to Division Two and City had signed John Charles from Roma for £25,000. The so-called Gentle Giant, on his debut, scored from 75 yards.

A season or two later, after an injury, he could not get back into the side. I recall sitting next to him in the stand as he glumly observed his teammates' endeavours. Generally, whenever this or that one made a blatant mistake he would remain silent, impassive; but when young Don Murray, who had supplanted him at centre-half blundered, he would groan audibly!

The Welsh crowds of thirty and more years ago remained relatively benign. Many had journeyed from the Valleys – blue-scarred coal miners in their flat caps among them. They have disappeared into the shiny grey photographic plates of a Welsh social history book. Decades have passed since the respectable, more posh spectators in the Grand Stand were astonished when one of their kind, sitting close to the directors' box, rose to his feet and screamed 'FUCKIN' UNGENTLE-MANLY BE'AVIOUR.' Even the disreputable gifted Welsh poet, John Tripp, who once accompanied me to Ninian Park, could only yell at the referee from time to time in a small voice, 'Go back to Hong Kong.' The referee hailed from Bristol so perhaps it was the rhyme of Hong and Kong that so entranced my companion. Then the crowd never cried out, as they regularly do now, 'THE REFEREE IS A WANKER.' Masturbation was still a taboo word.

I did eventually switch my season ticket seat from Block C to the present Block D. In my old seat, no spectator experiencing an oral orgasm would ejaculate boiled sweets on to the back of my neck; but a new pipe-smoking ticket holder parked himself next to me. I had only recently given up smoking myself. I did not wish to inhale second-hand tobacco smoke relentlessly through ninety minutes. Besides, another season ticket holder nearby irritated me by hurling abuse, week after week, at one particular player. First his wrath lasered on Derek Showers, a somewhat clumsy centre-forward. 'YOU ARE A SHOWER, SHOWERS. CRAAAP.' When Showers was dropped from the team he chose his next victim, the central defender, Albert Lamour, whose ability to kick into touch could have been the envy of many a rugby player. Almost every time Lamour received the ball he would be ready with his monotonous, repetitive, snarled abuse: 'YOU CART-'ORSE YOU. CRAAAP.'

It is customary to upbraid the referee's apparent diabolism. How often have I listened to the Ninian Park grumble: 'It's always an uphill struggle. We never 'ave a Welsh ref, see. Always a prejudiced Englishman.' But choosing to scapegoat one of our own players so regularly annoyed me. The following season I breathed the fresher air of Block D and now I still sit there next to a pleasant schoolteacher whose only unfavourable habit is to favour me charitably with an occasional religious tract.

True, at certain key matches, against Swansea for example, I sometimes believe that that Block C Ku Klux Klan-like character who needed to focus on a victim, has been cloned and cloned and cloned again. Quitting Ninian Park there have been occasions when I needed to move quickly to the safety of my parked car because of a sudden stampede of agitated running feet, raw shouts of rival supporters, over-alert policemen and police dogs barking. But the first time I encountered *real* malignant crowd menace was in the 1970s at a Millwall away match.

Even before the game began a whole mass of razor-headed yobs began to scream in unison, 'KICK THEIR FUCKIN' 'EADS IN, KICK THEIR FUCKIN' 'EADS IN.' They brandished their right fists rhythmically to this threatening cry which was orchestrated by no evident Oswald Mosley. To be sure, I had experienced milder displays of mindless crowd aggression but this was something else. Crowd rage. After the game that cancerous destructive violence metastasised around and about the mean streets of Cold Blow Lane.

Nowadays, unalloyed mass frenzy, barely suppressed, has ceased to be remarkable at soccer games. These battalions of ranting, lead-irritable, broken-homed, frustrated youths are but a legacy and symptom of our unhealthy, uncaring Thatcher-fashioned society where even TV football is stolen from the people by the fattest cats of this world. May they all drop dead.

Still, lethal crowds or not – and, fortunately, mostly not at Ninian Park – I enjoy my Bluebird Saturday afternoons. I like joining the crowds converging with sanguine expectation towards the turnstiles of the City ground. Men and blue-jeaned youths mainly, some wearing blue and white Cardiff City scarves or sponsored T-shirts, all walking purposefully in the same direction past the stragglers outside the Ninian pub, past the waiting, stern, distrustful police and their vans, to pass under the shabby railway bridge into Sloper Road itself with the looming stands and high, unlit floodlights of Ninian Park.

I feel the same old pleasurable anticipation as I take my place in Row M, Block D. No brass band entertains the relatively sparse spectators but the tannoy inaudibly gives out the team changes in what sounds like Serbo-Croat. No matter, I look towards the Grangetown Stand and I see a prewar boy who answers to my name. I hear him singing, 'Roll along, Cardiff City, roll along, to the top of the League where you belong. With a little bit of luck, you'll win the FA Cup, roll along Cardiff City, roll along.' But now a 1997 whistle blows. Car-DIFF. Car-DIFF.

the married man

EMMA LINDSEY

Paul Mortimer is a family man, his wife Sharon and four children rather than his team are his best friends and because of that he's had to make tough choices. A choice when he was at Aston Villa to put his family first. Now he is a Charlton midfielder. Of course there are regrets, it's torn him up, but he's reluctant to voice them. Instead a catalogue of injuries has made itself clear.

Injury. It could be his middle name. He jokes about it but you can see it hurts. There isn't much of him that hasn't been ripped up: Achilles, hamstring, lower back, knees, you name it, he's had jip with it. Why? Well the physios reckon there could be a few reasons. Diet maybe. There have been occasions, because he's coming home at odd hours out of kilter with the kids' meals and Sharon's been too knackered from rushing around all day carting them to and from school, gymnastics, drama lessons, Brownies, that Paul has gone down the road for a kebab and chips. It's not what you want really. Sharon dunks a herbal tea bag and offers me skimmed milk with my ordinary tea 'because we're trying to be more careful with the diet'. Recently he's been compelled to hire a fitness consultant who's made him buy loads of vitamins. He should have been doing that from the off. Perhaps he's been getting the wrong sort of advice, leaving him never fully recovered from one injury to the next. Good player, bad legs.

'On average I've played three games in a row before getting

injured. I went nineteen games without injury two seasons ago then snapped my Achilles,' he says.

'Next season he's got to really stay injury free,' says Sharon, if he is to have any solid hope of furthering his career.

'Football is a release and when you're injured there is none. I've been under pressure from my club this year and when you come home there is still pressure.'

'While he's injured, some Saturdays you don't know what to do with yourself,' says Sharon. 'I would rather go to football while Paul would rather not.' He sometimes gets cranky.

Football just reminds him of what he's not able to do. 'I snapped my Achilles and I had five months before my current contract with Charlton was finished. I was worried then but the club offered me a new deal because I had played well before the injury. My football seems to look after itself.' Counting his blessings – sometimes he prays in the bath – he says firmly: 'All the injury and illness makes your family life stronger.'

But it seems an unhappy trade-off underpinned by a huge potential for resentment. In those moments when the mind wanders idly, how to keep from exploring hypothetical avenues? Sharon, who admits she finds it hard to sit still, in the pause that follows his comment stops fiddling about with the dishwasher to offer a tour of their home. 'This is the first place we've furnished ourselves,' she says, brightly. Slightly embarrassed she confesses to having 'someone to clean once a week', as if it implied airs and graces above herself. Going upstairs, the wall is punctuated with big framed portrait photographs of Michael the baby, Courtney, 4, Hollie, 7, and Lataanya, 12. In the living room there is an oil painting of Paul in his kit which Sharon got done from a photograph for a Christmas present. That, his England Under-21 shirt in a Perspex frame and a couple of team photos, are the only visual clues to his career. (Dean Holdsworth has a whole room dedicated to his.) The children, strikingly beautiful and remarkably obedient to instructions not to disturb the grown-ups downstairs, are gyrating to the Spice Girls video. Michael, in a fat nappy, with a bottle planted in his mouth, gazes up at them absorbed.

Their house in a fairly dull, comfortably-off part of Surrey isn't what you would call posh. Sharon is keenly aware that they have four bedrooms, though. 'We're not flashy,' she says. Outside there's no sports car nor half-acre of garden, just the dustbin and a child's bike. She has made an effort to keep them all ordinary. 'My life wouldn't be different if he played in the Premiership because I wouldn't let it,' she says. On second thoughts, though, she wouldn't mind a second car. 'I'd still go down to football in my jeans – unless we were going out after. A couple of times we've gone in the snow and I've had to buy bovver boots, there's no way I'm going to stand there in a skirt and tights and freeze. As long as you're not really scruffy. The first time I went to Charlton, my mum and dad came too, I was in my jeans and the directors wanted to meet the wives. My mum said, "She can't meet them, look at her," but Paul insisted.'

Sharon and I recall our lunch with two wives of Wimbledon players, Samantha, since jilted by Dean Holdsworth, and Maxine, married to John Goodman. Turned out in designer garms, the Wimbledon wives swished into the restaurant with recently acquired self-importance. Sam and Maxine got on well, exchanging chat about nights out at Tramp and Langan's, thinking nothing of ordering champagne and the priciest dishes on the menu. Sharon dressed more casually, ordered pasta and, tiring of the fight to join in their conversation, settled for showing photographs of her brood and listening. It was interleague snobbery in full effect. No surprise then that she hasn't heard from them since. 'Not really my sort,' she says diplomatically, now back in the comfort of her kitchen. For a start, unlike them, she loves football – at the end of the kitchen counter a portable telly is always tuned to a match. She pauses mid-sentence to wince as Middlesbrough's relegation is sealed. 'When I was a kid I used to give my brothers money to let me play with them in the park.' Now she is just a spectator in the kitchen – her favourite room – while Paul watches something else on TV upstairs.

'My favourite team is Liverpool because they pass the ball around,' she says. 'I'll stand doing the ironing while I watch a game.'

Not much short of going into labour would keep her away from football. 'Lataanya was three weeks old when I took her to her first match. We'd take a packed lunch, go down on the train. I had Hollie on the Friday before a game with Oxford. Paul was at the birth, he'd been up all night and because he was so tired he scored an own goal. It had been one-all.' She has quite a few opinions about his game too, although she says: 'I don't give him advice.'

Paul gruffly interrupts: 'Because she doesn't know what she's talking about.' It's all right, he says, they give each other stick all the time. 'It's how footballers are,' he explains, before nipping out to take Courtney back to school after lunch. He says he's glad Sharon takes an interest.

When he is there, Sharon is happy just to listen to him. Once he's gone she can't wait to talk. 'He always asks me how I think he played. I do always say he's not greedy enough with the ball. There's been times he's had the ball and he should go for goal himself. He's too worried about other people's games. But I say to him, "Other people aren't going to be looking out for your career." He's played left-back a few times which he doesn't mind but I do. When he's in midfield he can be an exciting player. Defence to me is boring but if he can play there it might help extend his career, he won't be doing so much running up and down.'

When he's not playing he often doesn't have the heart to watch football. 'Sky have killed it through overkill. Who wants to see Carlisle versus Fulham?' And as for going to games – no way. 'The bar is crowded with hangers-on. At least if I watch on TV if it gets boring I can flick channels,' he says with more than a degree of disenchantment. Presumably it wasn't always like this.

'He's no different now to how he was at sixteen,' she thinks. That's how old he was when they met – she was twenty. 'He was an apprentice at Fulham. I was involved with someone else. For a long time Paul and I were just friends. His career has just grown with us really.'

He remembers: 'Fulham let me go because they said I was too small so I went to work in a bookshop in Fleet Street earning £150 a week. Sharon was earning more than me.' Then out of the blue Fulham asked him to play for them one Saturday against Charlton. 'I nearly didn't because I was so fed up with them but I decided to go ahead, played really well to prove a point and was then asked to join Charlton. I could have just stayed on the bus and things would have been very different.'

She says: 'When he started at Charlton the money was brilliant. We got our first mortgage on an ex-council house in Tooting. We still have it.'

His parents weren't too happy about him marrying a white woman. Sharon recalls: 'I already had Lataanya from my previous relationship so my parents couldn't really say much about it. My mum couldn't understand him at first. He has a footballer's sense of humour. My mum and dad bought my wedding dress but they weren't that happy about him being black. Paul's mum wasn't going to come to the wedding. When it came to the wedding a lot of his family didn't turn up. But it didn't spoil our day. Friends lent us their apartment in Spain for a week for our honeymoon and his mum looked after Lataanya.'

Not ideal but they made the best of it. Paul played excellent football, they did a lot of work to their house, then, 'the day after we'd finished painting – we hadn't even sat down in it together – he went up to Villa to have talks. At that time Sheffield United were interested and West Ham.'

'My manager didn't want me to go to Villa,' said Paul, but he went anyway.

'We didn't realise how different it was going to be until we got there,' says Sharon. 'The money was unbelievable, the size of the crowds at the matches, everything.' Paul's eyes light up momentarily. 'It was brilliant. Until I fell out with Ron Atkinson. In the first five games I was playing really well, set up a few goals and that. Then suddenly I was told I wasn't good enough after we rowed about accommodation.' One of the conditions of the transfer was that the club would fit them up with a furnished house. It never happened. It all became a struggle.

Sharon purses her lips as Paul launches into a monologue, the memories of how it all went pear-shaped painfully fresh.

'The whole eight months we were there we got shunted between hotels. Well, you can imagine with two kids under five, it was no joke. We were living out of suitcases. The kitchens would close and there would be nothing to eat, nowhere to warm the baby's bottle. Sharon had to manage on her own, because we were away a lot. I had a word with Atkinson about it and he told me to take the kids to McDonald's.

'I'd gone to them for £500,000 but I was treated abysmally. At half-time he'd have a go at me, contradicting his own instructions. The coach Andy Gray told me not to worry about him. Every day during training I would get called into his office for a bollocking. It became a joke with the lads.' He thought about fighting back but saw what happened to another player who did. 'Atkinson took his car away from him and made him come to training on a bike; he was pulled out of the side and ostracised by everyone else.'

People have said since that he couldn't take the pressure. 'But I could have stuck it out if I'd been single, I'd have fought on. Leaving Villa was a family decision. I had to think of Sharon and the kids.' Unbidden and probably unwanted, there is a note of wistfulness in his voice. 'It was a tough decision. Villa was the big time. Everyone knew who you were, it was flattering. It was a great feeling having got to the top. We had a coach for the first team squad, mobile phones, waitresses, the lot. I had achieved what I set out to do.' Villa let him go but he didn't want to leave. Even from a distance it feels sad.

Many of us start out with dreams of being the best at something. But all too often aspirations get shelved, because fear, bad luck or commitments get in the way. Followers of fate can take comfort from believing that what they wanted wasn't what life had planned. The rest are burdened with the task of keeping bitterness at bay. Success is handed to those standing in the right place – no matter how they get there – at the right time, with the single-mindedness to forsake all others in its name.

Paul folds and refolds a napkin then brushes invisible crumbs off the table and sighs. Sharon sits quietly. She would love him whatever he did, even if it were sweeping the streets. Then she finds something to say: 'It was nice to come back to London. Crystal Palace got us a house within a fortnight.'

But Paul hated it, pulls a face: 'I was depressed big time. I didn't want to be there. I told Steve Coppell I didn't like the sort of game they played.' Hardly a good start, he now realises. 'It was really cliquey and I suppose my feelings showed in the way I played. I was in a mess really. Football went from being something I loved to being a day job. I just thought about the money. It was like an eighteen-month prison sentence.' It's as if there aren't enough ways for him to describe just how bad he felt. In a gesture of solidarity Lataanya sulked for months, chucked her cherished Aston

Villa tracksuit in the bin and refused to go to a single Palace game.

It was tough on Sharon. 'Whenever I asked him if he was OK, he'd say nothing was wrong but I knew he was down. He'd snap and had no patience with anyone. I went through a couple of months when I thought, "This isn't the man I married." '

It was a crisis time. Paul's religion helped a bit but, 'it was mainly the kids that got me through it. Coming home to them I couldn't stay down for too long.' What really got to him more than anything else was being left out of the side, becoming a mere squad player. 'It was an insult, it was a complete waste of time in my career.' It was particularly hard after the bright lights of Villa. 'But through all the slaps in the face you have to stay ultra confident. Once you've signed that contract there's no going back.'

With the end of the season, and Paul's decision to turn down another contract, came a merciful end to the months of abject misery.

'Money isn't a big thing between us,' says Sharon, so the drop in salary when he went back to Charlton wasn't an issue. 'It means he's home a lot more too.' That doesn't always translate into more time spent with the family, he admits: 'During the summer holidays she has to go and visit people on her own. I can't take the kids out because I am training and I'm no use to anyone. One time I'd been running all day to the point of exhaustion. I got home and rested for twenty minutes and then we had to walk two or three miles to the park and I have never been so tired. I swore I would never do it again.'

It was tough for him coming back. 'In this game you don't go back. So to be at Charlton again was a comedown. In football there's nowhere to hide. I had to take people saying I wasn't cut out for the big league.' But at least, says Sharon, 'We knew everyone here.'

Paul agrees half-heartedly. 'First Division is great,' he says, trying and failing to convince either himself or me. Then it slips out: 'It's horrible in the First Division, it's not enjoyable it's not . . . how shall I put it . . . a high standard . . . But then the Premiership isn't the highest standard. The players have an inflated opinion of themselves because they immediately get a higher international profile no matter how well they're actually playing.' Finally he claims: 'I would be a better player at a higher level.' His expression betrays a flash of annoyance at finding he's inadvertently justifying himself. He's above that.

Sharon's one complaint is the club's lack of interest in the players' wives. 'We could do with having a crèche and an invite to the Christmas do.'

'You should get a job – anything, shift work, I don't know – then go to your own do,' says Paul. 'I keep telling her they don't have dos for housewives. She should get herself out of the house.' She says she doesn't feel confident. She's been out of it too long. He gives up again, puts a scone in the microwave.

The club had a celebration recently at the Cafe Royal but the wives weren't invited. 'We don't exist,' she says. That's a common complaint among footballers' wives. But it could be worse. Sam Holdsworth had complained – and as it turned out with due cause – about Wimbledon's pre-season training camps abroad being 'thirty good-looking blokes on a two-week jolly-up, basically. You know what men are like.' Temptation lurks in a lycra dress.

Sharon couldn't really sympathise. 'I don't have that problem. I don't think I could live like that, feeling I had to watch my back all the time. Paul isn't like that.' He doesn't go on the jolly-ups.

'The white boys hang out together,' he says. 'We get on as teammates but that's as far as it goes. There is a sheep mentality in football and if you don't go along with everyone else you've got a chip on your shoulder or you're a troublemaker.' Like the time he wouldn't go with Palace to South Africa, and he'd had to explain to one black teammate what apartheid was.

'I'm not a big drinker. But in clubs where blacks are the minority you have to make the effort to socialise, otherwise you are seen as having a problem.'

Sharon on the other hand doesn't really think about race. 'I suppose a lot of the white players and their wives do go out together but we don't get invited, so maybe colour has been a problem.'

'Definitely,' said Paul. 'Religion, race and politics are never mentioned in football because it causes arguments. Football still is a white man's game right the way through and it's got worse. I saw it when I was an apprentice but I didn't understand it. But as a black player you have to be better to prove them wrong.'

So for lots of reasons they have cultivated a social network outside football. Derek Quigley, youth development officer at Fulham now in his sixties, and Ray Harford are two of Paul's closest friends. 'I like to be with the family, really,' says Sharon. 'To me going out is going to the pictures and a restaurant.'

'When we go out I always have to suggest the place,' says Paul.

'Well, he knows from the lads where to go out,' says Sharon. 'A couple of times we've been out and it's pure posing – like the time at Stringfellows – and I'm just not interested.'

'That's part of the whole celebrity football scene which isn't my scene either, it just makes me laugh. But she gets intimidated,' counters Paul, rolling his eyes. 'I like to talk to people. I could spend the whole night just talking.'

But back to the race issue, because it is one. 'They see you as a threat if you're black and you have knowledge about the game. My first time at Charlton I got a lot of abuse. I had fights and rows with players. I was told I was sensitive and over-reacting.

They call it industrial language.' At the end of the day you just get on with it.

Reluctantly, because she would follow him to the ends of the earth, Sharon admits that some things do bug her. 'He doesn't get bank holidays off, or Christmas Day. He hasn't got weekends free so what you can do as a family is limited.' It could be very lonely. The way Susie Barnes described marriage to Liverpool's John as 'one long wait'; when things got so bad she just couldn't hack it anymore up north and the couple separated.

Sharon can't understand that. For her going to matches redefines their relationship, strengthens it: 'I get a funny feeling in my stomach. I'm on edge the whole time. When he scores a goal it's brilliant. I'll jump out of my seat cheering, especially if he's had a bad game the week before. I feel really proud to think that's my husband. Sometimes it's still hard to believe he plays football, that he's actually doing what he always said he wanted to do.' From the shine in her eyes, just describing it makes her fall in love with him all over again. Clearly she adores him. 'Whether he's playing Premier or First Division he's done very well for himself.' If only she could convince him of that, the ties that bind him might not feel so uncomfortably tight.

marco's room

HUGO BORST

Today Van Basten will tell her that it is exactly 30 years ago that he sat on her stomach to squeeze Marco out. Marco just wouldn't come, and in the end Van Basten pushed him out of his wife himself. It was a difficult birth, harder than the first two. Van Basten will also tell her that it is exactly 30 years ago that he sat on her stomach to squeeze Marco out. Marco just wouldn't come, and in the end Van Basten pushed him out of his wife himself. And he will tell her that it is Marco's birthday today. He has turned 30.

And tomorrow, tomorrow Van Basten will have been married 39 years. Tomorrow he will tell her that they have been married to each other for 39 years. She will say, 'Oh yes', and forget it immediately. He will repeat it a little later; she will say 'Oh yes' again and forget it immediately. Browsing in old copies of women's magazines, she will remark that smoking damages the health, and will advise him to give it up. In the evening in front of the television he will repeat another couple of times that they have been married 39 years.

Yesterday Liesbeth called, Marco's wife. This has become a kind of tradition now that Marco doesn't play anymore. That way it's still a bit like drinking coffee in Milan on Sunday morning. This afternoon he is going to telephone Marco, congratulate him on his thirtieth birthday and ask how his ankle is doing. But first someone is coming for the museum. Last week he gave someone else a tour, just like the week before, and next week someone is coming all the way from France or Turkey.

To the visitors, whom he strictly selects, Van Basten always says the same things. Life is an endless series of repetitions. So he tells them Marco's life story, and shows them the shirts, the prizes, the trophies, the photographs. Back upstairs they all ask the same questions, he gives the same answers he always does, and in between they always say what a nice view he has of the Amsterdam-Rhine Canal.

He no longer reads the names. After 18 years the passing barges hardly penetrate anymore, just as you usually don't hear the clock striking. Now that it's autumn, the cars on the horizon are driving from Utrecht to Amsterdam again. He usually does notice that, because he can see them between the ribs of the trees. Sometimes he sees himself driving, on the way to Ajax with two 17-year-olds on the back seat: Edwin Godee and Mar-e-co.

Only the sofa is new. Otherwise the room has remained as it was when they – first Marco and finally his wife – left home nine years ago; with its thick cream-coloured carpet, long since walked flat, the piano with the yellowed pages of sheet music and the table with the cloth on it. Van Basten spends each morning seated at the table: a cup of coffee, Camel filter cigarettes, an ashtray, a mid-market newspaper, the telephone that often rings, the view.

On the other side of the canal Marco is fleeing the scoundrels, Van Basten chasing after him. Marco is crying because they have kicked him again. Not once, but perhaps ten times. Van Basten catches up with him. Asks if he has completely lost his senses. Back! Now! He can see himself pointing. Go back to the club, back onto the pitch and kick back at the scoundrels. You'll never get there this way.

Marco turns round. Marco always listens to him. He wanted to play in midfield, with the game in front of him, where you get the ball more often, more freedom, fewer fouls, but Van Basten has forbidden this flight too. Marco, you're a striker. There are enough good midfield players, but few good strikers. And Marco always listens to him, always. Van Basten has been directing his youngest son's life since, sitting on her stomach, he squeezed the boy out of his wife. Sometimes Van Basten thinks he is being hard, but the drilling is necessary. Marco is his life's work.

We walk down two flights of stairs. At the entrance to Marco's room, Van Basten pauses by two pictures on the walls. Marco is cheering on one, crying on the other. 'That South American had kicked him twice in the groin. Dirty scoundrel. The other photograph represents the success he had, and this one the pain he suffered in his career. God, the pain that boy has had. Always when he took me to the airport after a game at San Siro, he'd complain about the stiffness of the joint and the pain.'

Van Basten expects me to ask if he would give his ankle for Marco; because other people ask that. Of course, he would answer, of course he would! If only he could. If only you could transplant ankle joints, just like kidneys and livers and hearts. Then Marco would stand up after every foul. But it turns out that everything of value is defenceless, that the scoundrels rule football, because referees are weak. 'It's sad that a boy who is not mean, who has so much skill, who can play football so beautifully, is the victim. Every Milan or Holland game I see now, I think for the whole 90 minutes: he could be playing here. When I see games from the past, when I see how good Marco was . . . I turn the TV off. I can't take it. It's a tragedy.'

Because Van Basten emphasises the last syllable, his remark takes on something unintentionally comical. I notice, incidentally, that Van Basten uses the past tense when talking about Marco. He doesn't believe it will ever again be Sunday afternoon for Marco, nor for himself either. Never again the fortnightly trip on Sunday 8.10 a.m. by KL341 to Milan, to be collected by Liesbeth and the grandchildren, a cup of coffee, to the stadium, holding Marco captive in his sights so that he doesn't get hurt, and afterwards being driven by Marco to Linate, in time for KL343, back in Utrecht at 11 p.m. Life is an endless series of repetitions.

'Marco wanted to go on until he was 35. Without injuries, without pain, my God he would have been great. Pelé, Maradona, Cruyff, people would have put him at that level,' he says as he opens the door to Marco's room.

In eleven square yards a thousand and one objects lie, stand, rest, show, shout, swear and blind. Among them:

almost 200 shirts, including the shirt of every Serie A club, shirts of Dutch clubs, shirts of various national teams, a shirt from the 1988 European Championship (number 12) and a shirt worn by Diego Maradona

about 12 pairs of shorts

various football socks

a captain's armband that belonged to Lothar Matthäus

a photograph of Ajax with coach Johan Cruyff and the European Cup-Winners' Cup (1987)

various other photographs

a painting of Marco in the AC Milan shirt

a (small) replica of the cup that Holland won at the 1988 European Championship

Van Basten depicted as the Pink Panther (porcelain)

The Golden Boot 1986 (highest scorer in Europe)

a crystal ball presented by Ajax ('1987 – Thanks and good luck')

a plaster bust of Marco

official accreditation World Cup Under-20s, 1983

a silver-plated cup won at table tennis, with the text 'TTV CJC club championship 78/79 2nd prize juniors'

four trophies for highest scorer of a season in the Dutch league, and two for the Italian league

two crystal wine glasses inscribed in gold letters with the words 'Bohemians Prague'

a koala bear sent from Australia

silver-plated cup: 'first prize boys' tournament '77 Unitas'

three trophies for European Player of the Year from *France Football*

two World Player of the Year trophies

an Italian comic book about Marco's life

14 thick scrapbooks with articles about Marco

one scrapbook with articles from the gossip press

It is cold and dusky in this room. But above all, it is restless. It is full here. And the shirts don't smell of sweat. It's not a boy's room at all, but an exhibition hall. Most football trophies are repulsive: they are too big, they shine falsely, they seldom represent what they stand for. In the prizes from *France Football* of which Van Basten is so proud, you see no elegance, no artistry, no beauty, no psychological warfare, no excitement, no provocations after a goal, no happiness, no power, no strength, no winner, no pain, no sweat; in nothing do you see that Marco was the best player in Europe then. It is strange that a thing like that is allowed to represent Marco's achievement. Only the silver European Cup with the big ears stands for the magic of the European Cup – and Marco won two of those – but of course it isn't here, not even a replica. And the World Cup is beautiful too, but Marco didn't win that, just because

Michels didn't make Cruyff Holland manager in 1990.

Only the frame of his bed, rebuilt by Van Basten because Marco was too tall, is still here. It stands on its side and serves as trophy cabinet. Its imprints in the carpet no longer exist. I can see no bookcase, and therefore no books. What did he use to read? Did he have *Charlie and the Chocolate Factory* here, *Asterix*, *Tintin*? Did his mother or his father read to him?

Van Basten, who suddenly looks very like Jackie Charlton, laughs, because Marco didn't like reading. 'He went to bed with a ball. That flat football was his cuddle toy. His life was a football. In the evening he wouldn't sleep until I'd talked to him about football for a bit. I didn't read to him. We always spoke about football. He'd sit on the edge of his bed and ask questions. When he was about eight, I brought in the blackboard, drew match situations in chalk, how he should make space for a midfield player's run. I told him what he was doing wrong on the pitch, how to play without the ball, because with the ball he could do anything anyway. When he was six I said to a friend: "He's going to play for Holland." '

I had hoped for the echo of Marco kicking a ball, for time that had stood still, for the pictures of film stars that still hang on the wall of Anne Frank's room, which say as much about Anne's history as any single page from her diary, I had hoped for a boy's room, not for this rather camp museum. Van Basten, God forbid, has destroyed with paint and brush the graffitoed practice wall in Marco's room. Marco used to shoot against it until it drove his housemates mad. Somewhere beneath that new layer is written what Marco thought, who he thought was good and who wasn't. We'll never know, and that's a shame. Judging by that one sentence written in thin, black, felt tip on the blotting paper on his desk, which I recently discovered (when I pushed aside a pile of interviews that Van Basten hasn't stuck in yet), a lot may have been lost: *I am the best, except for me.*

It came to Marco early. Humour. Irony. Arrogance. A massive truth. A ready made.

My desire for the clammiest kind of nostalgia is gratified after all: there are his football boots. Real weatherbeaten things that yearn for a lick of grease, but even more for Marco's supple joints. The sharp end of the studs pokes through the soles. Dry mud sticks to them, and blades of grass. 'No Golden Boot can beat that,' I say to Van Basten, but he doesn't hear me. He is sunk in thought. 'I wasn't always easy on Marco,' he says.

Van Basten is thinking of 1979, when Marco, by now playing for Holland Schoolboys, is told in a hospital after months of unbearable pain in the groin that he will become an invalid if he carries on playing football. At 20 he will be in a wheelchair. A professional career is out of the question. In the car they are silent for a couple of minutes. Then Marco asks: 'And now?'

'And now, and now? You just keep going on like this, kid.' Van Basten says this because he is filled with the dream that Marco will become a professional footballer, and an international. That Van Basten turns out to be right a couple of years later, that Marco doesn't end up in a wheelchair, that it was just growing pains, that it was the right decision to ignore the doctors, doesn't alter the fact that the risk he took at that moment was irresponsible. Afterwards, if it had all ended very badly, Marco might have reproached him for this decision, Van Basten sometimes thinks.

In one corner of the upturned bed, hidden beneath some magazines, lie three school files. I want to ask if these belonged to Marco, but Van Basten has looked at his watch and says that we must go upstairs now for a final cup of coffee, because he has to leave at 12.30, then he will be at his wife's at one, he will stay there until quarter to three, go back home, return to his wife's at quarter past five, buying food on the way to eat with her in front of the television at six, stay till quarter to ten, then go home. Tomorrow he'll visit her again. And the day after tomorrow. If he didn't go today, and he were to tell her tomorrow that they had had such a nice time yesterday, she would agree. But he goes. Because in the past he almost never saw her: at work during the day, and in the evenings and at weekends trainer, foot doctor, masseur and of course father to Marco. And because he has always told her that he will look after her until death.

And because – he says it with indignation – she is no rubbish bag that you dump outside the front door. And because she has always sacrificed herself for him and the children.

In the living room, seated at the table again, he does not notice that the water he is staring at has acquired a different colour because of the sudden change in the light. 'Marco swallowed up all the attention,' says Van Basten. 'Father was never home, and when we did all sit down at the table together, or on the sofa, the conversation was about football and about Marco. My other son played football too. Stanley often complained that I never went to watch him. He wasn't exploding with talent and I went to watch the best one. Football drove the other two berserk. If ever they had problems, at school or whatever, I didn't have time. Top-level sport comes at the expense of normal family life. Our whole family suffered. My family was dislocated by it. And on 16 October 1985, during Belgium–Holland, my wife hadn't felt well all day, she finally collapsed. In the weeks following she had a stroke which cost her her short-term memory. I think I have paid a very high price.'

Now that those two Sundays a month have also disappeared forever, all days seem even more alike. And yet there is nothing pathetic or tragic about Van Basten – quite the opposite. He is a proud, strong man. The heaviness of those sentences that have just fallen on the table like a brick do not point to a permanent sadness, or a dull acceptance. He is pleased that the sun is coming out: chances are good that he will be able to go for a half hour's walk with her.

It turns out that the boy's room contains a real treasure after all: the school files. They are lying open on the table in front of us:

an anthracite-grey file with three stickers contains Marco's notes for the football season '80/'81 (the year that Marco played in the A1, the highest youth team, of his amateur club Elinkwijk), the season '81/'82 (his first season at Ajax) and the season '82/'83 (only a few pages)

a blue file with a sticker saying 'team Suzuki' contains Marco's notes for the '83/'84 season

a light-grey file with on its cover the word 'Biology' (inside a reference to Marco's school days and his first girl-friend: 'Anne is sweet after all! – When she is asleep'). It contains Marco's notes for the '84/'85 season

'There must be some notebooks somewhere,' says Van Basten. 'He kept records of his time in boys' football too. But I have no idea where they are.'

For every match Marco played for the Elinkwijk A1 team, he has recorded whether he played (or was injured) and whether he scored. Every week there is an updated league table, in which he has calculated matches won and lost, draws, goal difference and total goals for and against for every club in the division.

Texas – Ajax Reserves: 3–7

This must be his first match in an Ajax shirt. It is Sunday 2 August and Marco scores on his debut. Leafing through the pages you come across many forgotten young hopefuls. For every match Marco played for Ajax or a representative team, he has noted the date, the score, who played with him, and how many goals he scored himself. At the end of his first season with Ajax it turns out that in 44 matches for the A1, the reserves and the first team, Marco has scored 68 times. He often signs the pages with an autograph that long remains childish, is sometimes experimental, and later acquires its definitive shape. These are undoubtedly finger exercises for later, when he is famous.

In his notes Marco is succinct and sober. He ignores joy and sadness, appears interested in facts alone. Only occasionally does he elaborate. For instance:

> *Sunday 8 November 1981 KBV A1 – Ajax A1 0–3 Goals: 2 (jewels)*
>
> *Saturday 13 February 1982 Ajax Reserves – Heerenveen Reserves 7–0 Scored: 4. I substituted myself after 80 mins (cramp), but played brilliantly*
>
> *31–1–'82 Tournament Hannover. I played five minutes this tournament and therefore I hope the whole lot of them get a heart swelling!*
>
> *Wednesday 7 September 1983 Holland–Iceland 3–0 Debut in the NL team!*
>
> *in Groningen*
>
> *played well*
>
> *didn't score*

It is exciting to turn the pages with their *Gazetta dello Sport*-pink tint and to read the handwriting of a footballer who is already playing for his country, to allow his notes to evoke special matches in your memory. Such as the famous Ajax–Feyenoord of Sunday 18 September 1983. It finished 8–2, and apart from the arrow referring to his constant position changes with Jesper Olsen, Marco writes merely:

Scored: 3x

Marco refrains from comment, perhaps out of piety for his idol Johan Cruyff, who as a Feyenoord player was humiliated in the Olympic Stadium. Strangely, he also does not describe the lob with which he beat the Feyenoord keeper Joop Hiele.

The best page is the one which says:

Wednesday 12 October 1983
Ireland–Holland 2–3.
1st half: 4–4–2: 2–0!
2nd half: 4–3–3: 2–3!

Beneath the line-up, which has Gullit at sweeper and Ronald Koeman in midfield, he has noted only that he scored one goal. I can still see him standing on his hands after the winner. That evening was the birth of the Dutch team that won the European Championship five years later. On 13 May 1984 Ajax beats DS'79 7–2. Marco writes: *scored 5x. TOPSCORER of PREMIER DIVISION with 28. Johan Cruyff stops his career with Feyenoord today.*

One of the last pages of the light-grey file, one of the last notes he makes, a reference to the then Ajax manager Aad de Mos:

Tuesday 23 April 1985
FC Utrecht – Ajax 0–1
I reserve!! 'De Mos has never been in form'
Sunday 5 May 1985
Haarlem – 1–0
I reserve!

Beneath it Marco has written:

De Mos was relieved of his duties as manager of Ajax on 6 May!

Van Basten says that Marco recently had a look around his old room, for the first time in years, that he had never cared much about it, but that this time he suddenly said: 'Nice, isn't it, that I won all that.' It sounded as if Marco had decided for himself that his career was over. 'God, how I hope that he can walk properly the rest of his life. He's only 30. Marco has a whole life ahead of him,' Van Basten says seriously.

It's twenty past twelve. The guest is requested to take his leave. Just then I discover inside the anthracite-grey file a piece of paper on which is written in capital letter: FEINTS. Marco has numbered them from one to fourteen.

Van Basten throws the page a quick glance, vague recognition. 'He must have been 14, 15 years old then. I told you: the boy was obsessed. A fanatic. You can borrow the files for a while if you want.'

Marco's repertoire than consists of 14 feints, taken from players like Didier Six, Johan Cruyff and Ruud Krol right through to Utrecht amateur footballers such as Haub Mess, Marcel le Duc and someone called Pieter. Some of the feints are intelligible, others are described cryptically. They took him a long way. Even with that iron construction around his lower right leg, even with the pins in his bones, with gristle in the joint – with or without bone marrow – he has mastered all 14 feints. What is written here in child's handwriting is anchored in him forever. 'If the weather stays like this, we'll be able to go for a walk,' Van Basten remarks with satisfaction as he sees me out.

Translated by Simon Kuper.

referee

You made your way past the blazes and clamours of the black-
smith's shop to get to the village football pitch, where the local
team, the Gilmerton Drumbirds, called after a nearby pedimented
country house, turned out in a Newcastle strip of black and white
stripes, and where I played my first game on grass. Before that, it
had been the street, with pauses to let the cars through. I was one
of a straggle of minors who fawned on, while trying to tackle, a
boy wizard of the dribble, Bailie Hutchison, all swerves and flying
hair. The man in charge was a dark and dignified professional
centre-half, Baxter of Hibernian. To the south of us rose a
Midlothian hinterland and soccer heartland, composed of mining
villages with teams such as Newtongrange Star.

Hibs versus Hearts was the first of football's scenes of
contention which I was to witness. Part-Irish though I was, I
had no idea that there was a touch of Ulster here: that Heart of
Midlothian (their shirts a cardiac maroon) could be thought to
play for the Protestant Ascendancy, and that Hibs (green shirts
with white sleeves) had evolved from the exploited Irish presence in upcountry Midlothian which was established in the early
19th century. I just sort of supported Hibs, and admired their
star, the winger Gordon Smith, more handsome and even more
wizard than Bailie Hutchison. It's true that this Ulster stuff had
become more or less vestigial, and even the 30 years of trouble in
Ulster proper have failed to inflame it. They do things differently
in Glasgow, where Celtic and Rangers have yet to desert the

battlefield of the Boyne. I had a grandfather who played for Rangers, or so I have been anxious to believe. Not that I support the Protestant Ascendancy.

Baxter was both coach and referee. But I don't remember any bustling or intrusive decisions on his part, and I don't suppose we needed all that many decisions of any kind. Kids don't have much need of referees. Kids rarely foul; that comes with maturity. In this minimal approach to refereeing lay a wisdom which became clearer to me in years to come.

So much for my roots. Twenty-five years later, in the London of the Sixties, I played football with a dilettante team of journalists and others, called Battersea Park. On our chests a simple-hearted row of power-station smokestacks, black on white. One Sunday morning we made our way to a distant sports complex to play a team called Log Cabin, which could have done with a few sombrero'd outlaws on their chests. The team was made up largely of night-club bouncers. Given that there were these pirates on the park, the referee was a reassuring sight. On a shiny black blouse rested, on its string, a silver whistle. Nice shorts, plump knees, an air of frowning efficiency and lonely eminence. From the off, we were overpowered by trips, elbows. Our stars went out. The game played by Log Cabin was quite different from anything I'd ever seen. It was an education to watch these hard men devoting themselves in their maturity to foul play, and to winning that way. The referee's silver whistle soon fell silent, and we lost by a wide margin. I had discovered that when adults take the field you have to have referees who referee.

All this is a preamble to the assertion that both here and abroad, but especially here, it would seem, the game is being damaged by officious, excessive and creative refereeing. And it has never been worse, as far as England is concerned, than it was last season, 1996–97.

No referee can be expected to see everything that happens during a game. He is bound to miss things and to get them wrong. This suggests, or should suggest, that he'd do well to be modest in his interventions, that linesmen should be consulted far more often than they are, and that photography should be used, as in cricket and racing, when matters of life and death arise in important games. Referees urgently need to be told: where there is uncertainty, as there often is, don't intervene, don't penalise unless you really have to. Steer clear of penalty kicks. Give them only when you're unequivocally compelled to give them. At present, the defender is regularly the fall guy in 50/50 challenges, which are allowed to produce penalties and to decide games. When you or the linesman aren't absolutely sure that the ball has crossed the line into touch, for God's sake let the game go on. Let the player have the benefit of the doubt. Refs seem to find this hard to do – many of them, temperamentally, are stoppers.

Then there's this business of touching. There's no law in football against touching, though you'd think there was, to hear the cries that go up. If a player is going for the ball and an opponent is checked or bowled over as a result, no foul has been committed. But fouls are awarded in such circumstances all the time. Players can't play, or earn their living, except by going for the ball.

The concept of intention is another source of great misunderstanding on the part of the game's dogmatists, who talk as if intention were its foundation stone. This is one of those ideas in football which should be rated stultifyingly vague; another is the idea of 'interference with play' for determining the offsides referees love to give. 'What are they doing on the field if they aren't interfering with play?' asked Danny Blanchflower. A referee's assessments should be governed, not by any view as to intention, which is frequently debatable if not inscrutable, but by the notion of unfair advantage secured by a breach of the rules. No player deliberately fouls another in his own penalty area unless there is plainly no other way of preventing a goal or unless he believes that the referee has left the field.

Most fouls are accidents: this doesn't mean that most fouls should be ignored, but it does indicate that referees should be slower than they are now to treat players as guilty perpetrators of the fouls that have to be declared. One of the ironies of the current game is that the hard men and the crafty destroyers are seldom high on the list of those who are sent off. Meanwhile Gianfranco Zola of Chelsea, a marvellous and scrupulous player, having been struck in the face with no penalty imposed, is carded for then delivering back the ball to the opposition perhaps a little too vehemently. Free kicks have to be awarded for fouls that are likely to have been accidental: but it should be recognised that players have to try their best, and that they are like other people in not always intending or knowing what they are doing at any given point.

I'll turn to instances now, most of which, by the nature of such cases, are likely to provoke some degree of disagreement. My penalty isn't always going to be your penalty – which is one good reason for cutting back on game-deciding penalty decisions.

England began the Euro 96 tournament in unconvincing style, but were well on top of my native Scotland when, in his penalty area, their defender Tony Adams stuck out a leg to get at the ball, and a Scottish forward fell over the leg. This was declared a penalty. Adams is a bit rough and a bit clumsy at times, but he doesn't go about committing fouls in front of the referee a yard out from his goal-line. A footballer's foot can be quicker and subtler than the spectator's eye, but it would be daft to suspect this footballer of a scam on this occasion. The penalty kick (as unfairly awarded penalty kicks quite often are) was missed, and what bribing Tory MPs call natural justice was served. England went on to seal the game when the soccer journalists' perpetually deplorable and past-it Paul Gascoigne burst through and volleyed into the net. But the referee had done his best to produce an artificial, engineered result.

There's no trouble at all in naming more recent decisions of this kind; the spring of 1997 has been a particularly bad time for over-refereeing. In a friendly against Mexico at Wembley, England were regaled with a penalty when a Mexican defender was held to have tripped their captain, Ince, who helped to bring about the award with one of his many fits of hostile indignation. A ragged England won, spurred by the award. Having exulted over the goal, BBCTV's commentators discovered on a second look that the penalty had been a mistake.

In the FA Cup, Leicester were knocked out by a penalty award that was universally condemned. Worse was to come, however, in the semi-final, between costly Premier Division Middlesbrough, stiff with foreign talent, talented talent at that, and Second Division Chesterfield, who did well and went ahead – only to be shorn of their two-goal lead by two highly regrettable decisions. The Brazilian Juninho fell over, untouched by the Chesterfield defender who was penalised for bringing him down; and, without consultation with the linesmen, as far as I could tell, a good goal was disallowed, occasioning, said the *Guardian*, 'the sort of refereeing controversy which has plagued this season'. Predictably, Chesterfield lost the replay. But at least the result went the way the play did, though the same referee was in charge, and did manage to express himself by disallowing a perfectly good, not to say sparkling Juninho goal. Referees have been known to make amends for a wrong decision by leaning subsequently in the opposite direction, and this referee had accepted that the disallowed goal in the previous game had been a mistake. The BBCTV commentator hailed the decision to disallow the Juninho goal, apparently because of a possible jostle or shirt-pull elsewhere on the field, held no doubt to have 'interfered with play': but he was followed by a studio expert, Alan Hansen, who said that there wasn't anything wrong with it. And there wasn't.

When Liverpool played Arsenal, Robbie Fowler tumbled when his friend the Arsenal keeper dived for the ball. Fowler immediately sprang up to wave his hand in disclaimer: he hadn't been touched. He was both praised and blamed for this action, which was examined with the care that novelists give to questions of motive. The old master, endearing Jimmy Greaves, suggested that Fowler had taken a dive and repented. It must have been a lightning repentance – between the stirrup and the ground, as St Augustine used to say of such sudden changes of heart, with reference to the sinner who might be saved from perdition in the course of falling to his death from a horse. It's true that players are encouraged to fall in penalty areas, and often fall their way out of collisions. But the only intention on Fowler's part that could be clearly read on this occasion was the intention to indicate that no penalty offence had been committed. Elsewhere, shortly before this, having scored another of his goals, he'd bared his vest to display a legend which supported the locked-out Liverpool dockers. He was fined for that by the international football authorities. I am surprised that the English Football Association didn't fine Fowler for signalling that he hadn't been fouled.

There's such a thing as under-refereeing too, though it does less harm, by and large. Referees can be ruinously officious, and they can be ruinously lenient. When Wimbledon played Sheffield Wednesday this spring, they'd been on a long winning streak which had impressed commentators without making them interesting to watch. In the first half-hour three injuries were inflicted. Wednesday's key forward Carbone was grounded, and was able to resume only at half-power. And two other prominent Wednesday players were stretchered off with ankle injuries, having been on the end of tackles. Deliberate? Wimbledon have a reputation for dangerous play, and their ex-player John Fashanu will long be remembered for the damage he did when he smashed his elbow into a Spurs defender's face. On this occasion none of the Wimbledon players responsible for what happened during the injury time that coincided with the first half-hour was penalised, and Wimbledon won.

The casualty rate went unmentioned, I think, by the BBC television soccer experts who discussed what took place on that Flanders field. Everyone knows what these armchair referees like to say. They like to say that so-and-so will be 'very disappointed' with that miss, that some team is failing to 'push forward'. The most rewarding of the match commentators, to my mind, is John Motson, who knows and loves the game, and who once pointed out his father in the stand, while Barry Davies is the most supercilious, and Alan Hansen the most judgemental, of television's football experts, in or out of the studio. For Hansen, no goal is ever scored which is not the fault of some defender. He is as infallible as the Pope used to be, and as referees continue to be, though he is a little apt to be wrong at half-time, when he is fond of predicting that the losing team will go on losing, failing to push forward and experiencing disappointments. His losing teams have a way of winning.

With such powers of reproof available to the studio and the commentary box, you might hope that more could be done to correct the more disastrous mistakes made by football's on-the-field infallibles. Commentators and studio experts have a better view of the game in many of its aspects, and the experts have hindsight to assist them. Both sets of people do make criticisms of referees, but they haven't tried hard enough to impose a check on the present wave of excessive and wrongful refereeing. It may be that they defer too much to the official in charge, that like calls to like in the matter of knowing better than the players. Both sets of people bear a certain resemblance to literary critics, who are generally so keen to blame their writers and to be disappointed by their performances.

Referees should look out for dangerous play and for the seeking of unfair advantage. They should beware of the intentional fallacy. And they should award very few penalties. They have a difficult job – they ought not to be shouted at and reviled. But ever since the new stringency which was ordained for the 1990 World Cup, where it did succeed in reducing the incidence of violent play, they have been getting above themselves. And there are those of them in England who've been bringing the game into disrepute. That last expression is ironically intended – it has long been used by po-faced officials engaged in the blaming of players. But it isn't altogether inappropriate here. These referees have certainly been causing confusion. The game depends on the integrity of its goals, on the confidence that players have not been bribed to concede them, and that they have not been manufactured by the man in black.

southgate, philippa and the buffaloes: a diary of euro 96

SIMON KUPER

17 May 1996 I used to think that if you wanted to be a journalist you had to be able to write well. Thank God that has nothing to do with it. This morning in the tube I run into Henry, whom I know from Arsenal matches. I tell him that my newspaper, the *Financial Times*, won't be covering Euro 96.

'Then you should cover it for Agence France Presse,' says Henry. 'A friend of mine works there.'

18 May Henry's friend Niall introduces me to his boss, Monique. Thanks to my ten years of growing up in a small Dutch town, I am to report on Holland's Euro 96 matches in English. But I also have to be able to speak French, so that I can talk to my colleagues.

'How good is your French?' asks Monique.

'*Bien*,' I say. '*Très bien*.'

31 May The England team damage a table and two TV sets in an aeroplane. It is generally agreed that Gazza should be banned from Euro 96.

I appear on a television show to say he shouldn't be banned. I quite like Gazza – the story, for instance, about his night on the town with Gary Lineker in London during their Spurs days. At the end of the evening they got into a bus at Trafalgar Square and Gazza asked the driver: 'Can you take us to Lineker's house?'

The driver explained that Lineker's house was not on his route. But if the other passengers agreed, he was happy to take them there.

Gazza asked the passengers: 'Shall we go to Lineker's house?'

'Yeeessss!' everyone shouted. And on the way there Gazza led them in a singalong of 'We're All Going on a Summer Holiday.'

I think the story is apocryphal.

In the audience at the show tonight is Charlie George, the former Arsenal player. Afterwards I ask him whether footballers drank less in his day.

'Same as now,' says George, and orders another one. George has become a nerd with a computer programmer's haircut and enormous spectacles.

1 June I call Philippa. 'Did you see me on TV last night?' I ask.

'No,' she says.

'But I specifically told you to watch at 10.30.'

'I turned on the TV at 10.32, but by then they were already on to the next guest.'

Philippa tells me that some Euro 96 matches are going to be played on Clapham Common, near her house. Someone has told her so. She is looking forward to it.

7 June Euro 96 kicks off tomorrow!

8 June When Euro 96 kicks off I am standing at a garden party in Cambridge. I find the nearest student dorm, where a group of 18-year-olds is watching TV.

'Can I climb in through the window?' I ask.

'You can use the door if you want to,' they say.

Gareth Southgate heads the ball into the feet of a Swiss player, who shoots against Stuart Pearce's hand. Switzerland get a penalty. The 18-year-olds chuckle.

> *They've seen it all before*
> *They just know, they're so sure,*
> *That England's going to*
> *Throw it away*

Switzerland score. I am sorry that Southgate made the error. I know Southgate: we met on a freezing cold day at the Aston Villa training ground three months ago, when he struck me as a very polite boy with a big nose. At one point the Villa coach, Paul Barron, a Superman-figure, decided to measure our body-fat percentages. Southgate took off his shirt and let Barron attach what looked like electrodes to him.

It turned out that only nine per cent of Southgate's body consisted of fat. Ugo Ehiogu, his teammate, has a freakish body fat ratio of seven per cent.

'I'm glad I'm not that thin,' I said. I took off my shirt and Barron inspected my stomach.

'Maybe we should just use the slap test,' he said.

'What's the slap test?'

'Slap you in the stomach and see how long it shakes.'

Southgate was still lying on the floor attached to electrodes. 'Paul,' he said mildly, 'this bloke has only come round to write an article.'

My body fat ratio was 16 per cent. Southgate told me not to worry. 'Just go to the gym for three hours every night for the rest of your life and you'll be fine.'

Southgate wanted to be a journalist, and we agreed that he would write a Euro 96 diary for the *Financial Times*, but somehow it never happened.

★ ★ ★

9 June Today I'm going to watch all three matches. I telephone Philippa. 'Tell you what. You come over and we'll watch Euro 96 in the living room all day.'

'No,' says Philippa.

'OK,' I say.

Instead we go to Regents Park and lie in the grass. It's nice weather, and we read the Sunday papers and wander around and talk about life. Now, I may have my faults, but I know what women want. They want to watch football. And it just so happens that Germany/Czech Republic is about it kick off. So we leave the park and find a table in the Allsop Arms.

Germany score. Philippa has begun talking about nice-looking footballers.

'Who's the nicest-looking footballer in the England team?' I ask. Philippa chooses Ryan Giggs.

Germany score again. Philippa is reading the newspaper. 'Those Euro 96 ads are clever,' she says.

'What do you mean?'

'Well, sleep football, eat football, drink Pepsi Cola. It really sticks in your mind.' She asks when the last Euro 96 was played.

It's half-time, Ruud Gullit appears on TV, and Philippa becomes dreamy. Then she walks out of the pub and goes home.

No problem. An hour and a half later it's Denmark/Portugal and I am in the Allsop Arms again, this time with my housemate Shilpa. Shilpa hadn't planned to watch Euro 96, but she likes it.

'I like all the Portuguese players, most of the Italians, some of the Spaniards and a couple of the Dutch,' she says.

'What about England?'

'Oh no,' says Shilpa. 'They're all working-class boys who go out with porn stars. Foreign players are probably just the same, but because you don't know that for sure they retain an air of mystery.' Before the Gascoigne era, she adds, England players were sexy.

Shilpa tells me what's sexy about football:

— 'When they fall. Tumbles are very pleasant. It's the vulnerability of those strong men.'

— 'This might be a bit kinky, but I like it when they hug each other.'

— 'Shinpads. Footballers have very thin calves, but the shinpads make them look a bit fuller.'

— 'Portuguese footballers.'

Just then Joao Pinto appears on the screen. I say, 'You've got to admit that he's a very ugly guy,' and simultaneously Shilpa says, 'He's the best looking man in the game.'

'But he looks like a monkey.' Joao Pinto blows out snot through his nostrils.

'He has come-to-bed eyes. Are you writing this down? I hope Joao Pinto reads your diary.'

I tell Shilpa that the entire Portuguese squad reads *Perfect Pitch*, on orders from the coach, Antonio Oliveira, who appears on the screen at that point looking uncannily like Groucho Marx. Artur Jorge, the Swiss coach, and Guus Hiddink, the Dutch coach, also look like Groucho Marx.

10 June In the train to Birmingham for Holland/Scotland I meet Hugh McIlvanney. The two parts of his tie are pointing in opposite directions, he is smoking a £6 cigar, and it is only ten in the morning. On the way McIlvanney tells me about great footballers and managers. He thinks they come from a different planet and should be treated accordingly.

'I remember Frank McGhee asking Alf Ramsey, "Mr Ramsey, could you perhaps explain why you are playing Martin Peters, and how he will strengthen the team?"

'And Alf said: "No." '

McIlvanney talks about Bobby Moore, Tostao and Ruud Gullit. He tells me about George Connolly, a brilliant player who lost the European Cup final with Celtic in 1970, forgot how to play football overnight, and became a truck driver.

He tells me about a young journalist who told him recently that a game had been 'very intriguing'. McIlvanney waves his cigar about. 'When I go to a football match I don't want to be intrigued! I want to be moved!'

When we arrive in Birmingham McIlvanney is fast asleep. He has probably been to Villa Park 30 times in the last 30 years, but he still has no idea where it is. Euro 96 is the worst organised tournament I have ever been to, so there are no signs pointing the way. But football fans have a sort of homing instinct for football grounds, and everyone walks straight there.

McIlvanney is worried for Scotland.

'This is not the best Dutch team of all time,' I reassure him.

'No,' he says, 'but it is the worst Scottish team.'

The game ends in a 0-0 draw. I write a match report for Agence France Presse that will reach large swathes of Asia, and then go to the press conference and discover that I am the only person in Europe who didn't see John Collins handle the ball on his goal-line in the fifth minute. Does this invalidate my report?

Nah.

Holland played fairly well and so did Scotland. The Dutch players say they played extremely well. Richard Witschge is the first Holland player I ever speak to. He too thinks he played extremely well.

I start to learn the rules of the 'mixed zone', the tent where journalists are allowed to shout questions at passing footballers after matches. The aim is to get the footballer to stop and begin talking to you. These are the Commandments of the Journalist in the Mixed Zone:

— Tell the footballer he has played brilliantly. 'A real shame they got that fourth goal. You were just starting to dominate the game.'

— Lend the footballer your mobile phone, so that he can phone home to say how well he has played, while you wrap your arm around him.

— Lend the footballer your wife.

— Shout, 'Great news about the Juventus offer!'

— Lengthily shake the footballer's hand. This not only expresses affection, but also prevents him from walking on without a brief struggle.

Several journalists, using a variety of these strategies, have cornered Ronald de Boer. 'Don't you think England played badly against Switzerland?' an English journalist asks him.

'Not at all,' replies De Boer.

The journalist walks away, and I ask De Boer in Dutch whether he thought England played badly against Switzerland.

'Yes, of course. Very badly.'

'So in English you say they were good, and in Dutch that they were bad?'

'Yes,' says De Boer.

I decide to tell McIlvanney. One day – perhaps somewhere in the Korean provinces in 2002 – he'll repay me. As mafiosi say, 'I don't do favours, I just collect debts.'

Journalists are complaining that the only Euro 96 freebie we have been given is a black plastic shoulder bag.

At the hamburger bar at Birmingham station the hamburgers have run out. The station is dirty and the bar is closed. The Dutch fans are being very cheery – if the world were destroyed by nuclear bombs the Dutch would be cheery – but you can see them thinking: 'Back home everything is better.'

I finally catch a train to Liverpool and congratulate myself on my debut in my fourth major football tournament. I want to be like Diego Lucero, the only person in the world in 1994 who had been to every World Cup. Lucero had nothing to say, but because he had seen every World Cup everyone kept interviewing him. Now he is dead, so he will probably miss the World Cup in France.

My first tournament was the 1988 European Championship. I was 18, and I had arranged a ticket for the final, Holland/USSR. I flew out to Munich on the morning of the match, with enough money to stay in a youth hostel for two nights and even to have something to eat every now and then.

In the bus to the stadium two men in green uniforms came up to me, one of them a fat man with a Hitler moustache and the other a slightly less fat man with a Hitler moustache.

'Ticket,' the slightly fatter man said. I gave him my ticket.

'Forty marks,' he said.

I hadn't stamped my ticket. 'I didn't know I had to,' I said.

'Those are the rules here,' the less fat man said. I began to cry a little.

I saw the match, slept in the station for two nights, and on Sunday evening bought myself a sandwich.

11 June   A company that runs public relations for Merseyside has invited me and ten other journalists to see Italy/Russia. The theory is that if they take you to a big match, you are more likely to write kind articles about them. Does it really work like that?

Yes of course it does.

Before the match we are given lunch at Anfield. We are having a nice time eating and chatting when suddenly two old men get up on a stage and start talking to us. They are Tommy Docherty and Emlyn Hughes. 'I'm sorry to interrupt your lunch,' says Docherty. He tells a couple of his most famous anecdotes and then some Scotland jokes. Because this is

Liverpool, he has thought up a local interest joke: 'If John Lennon had been shot at by a Scottish striker, he'd still be alive today!'

Emlyn Hughes says that playing for England used to make him feel proud.

At the game I sit next to Denise, a girl from the PR company. It's the first football match she's ever seen. And while I tell her what's happening on the pitch, I start to ask myself, Is football really that much fun? Because Denise desperately wants to like football. And Italy and Russia are quite good teams. And every now and then the match seems about to become interesting: a player beats his opponent, or gives a 20-yard pass, or sets up a one-two. But no sooner do things start looking up than there'll be a bad pass or a good tackle, and the excitement vanishes. I feel sorry for Denise.

12 June   'Burgcamp was good against Scotland, wasn't he?' Peter Aspden, our sports editor, asks me.

In fact Bergkamp played badly, but English fans can never accept that. Another friend of mine has told me that when Bergkamp fails for Arsenal it's because his teammates can't understand him. This man said: 'If Albert Einstein walked into your local pub and started explaining the relativity theory, no one would know what he was going on about. People might even think he was crazy. And it's the same with Burgcamp at Arsenal.' In England, admiring Bergkamp is seen as the mark of a higher sensibility, like enjoying ballet or the opera.

Journalists like big tournaments because they get to meet old friends from other countries and put the drinks on expenses. Tonight I meet Mark Gleeson, who has come over from South Africa for three days. We are sitting in a Spanish cellar bar, where the temperature is 33 degrees.

'Why have you come all the way from Cape Town just for three days?' I ask.

'Mastercard paid for my trip. They wanted me to give a seminar on African football for the European press.'

'Does the European press want to hear about African football during the European Championships?'

'No,' says Mark. 'The seminar has been cancelled.'

'So you've come all the way for nothing?'

'Well I did get the shoulder bag.'

13 June   I catch four hours' sleep. Euro 96 is getting to me. Before breakfast I write three previews of Holland/Switzerland for Agence France Presse. Then I go to the *FT*, pretend to work, and at three o'clock I take the train to Birmingham.

I am travelling with Peter Aspden and our former colleague Peter Berlin. Peter Berlin is very intelligent, but because he used to wear Bermuda shorts to work he was regarded so poorly at the *FT* that he wasn't given a career discussion for eight years.

A year ago he told the *Herald Tribune* that he was the *FT*'s sports editor. That was a slight exaggeration, although he did put together our weekly sports page. But the *Herald Tribune* thought: 'My God! Sports editor of the *Financial Times*!' and signed him up immediately.

A few seconds after the train leaves Euston the debate begins. Peter Berlin asks: 'What was the moment when English football began to deteriorate?'

The last time he asked this question, in a South London sandwich bar about a year ago, Peter Aspden shouted out: 'The moment that Bobby Charlton was substituted in Leon!'

And Peter Berlin had replied: 'That's exactly what I was going to say!' (Leon, quarter-final, World Cup 1970, 20 minutes left to play, and England are beating West Germany 2-0.

Ramsey substitutes Charlton to save him for the semi-final. Germany score three times.)

I remind Peter and Peter of this conversation. They have completely forgotten it. Peter Aspden says: 'This time I wanted to nominate the moment in the same match, with the score still 2-0, when Franny Lee steps over a shot from Martin Peters thinking that it's going in.'

But Peter Berlin disagrees. 'I disagree with the question,' he says.

'You asked it yourself,' we point out.

'I don't think English football has deteriorated.'

'Why not? You agree that it used to be good, don't you?'

'Yes.'

'And you agree that it's bad now?'

'Yes.'

'Well then it has deteriorated!'

'Not necessarily.'

Holland play badly and Switzerland play quite well. After an hour the score is still 0-0.

I start thinking about my life. I have hardly slept for a week, because besides Euro 96 I have a full-time job at the *Financial Times*. Philippa thinks I'm dull. I spend vast swathes of my time in the train to Birmingham. And what for? For this lazy, third-rate Dutch team. Then Jordi scores and I jump into the air, a solitary flying figure in the press stand, and hug my French colleague Arnaud.

15 June I live near Baker Street, the main tube link for Wembley, and so on match days the fans come and urinate against my house. Today it's England/Scotland. The bigger the match, the wetter our door.

'Handy, isn't it, if you don't live there?' I shout at one

middle-aged fan from my window this morning.

'It's perfect,' he says, zipping up his trousers.

I throw a mug at him but it misses, breaks on the bonnet of a Land Rover, and sets off the car alarm.

16 June Philippa and I are lying in the grass in Green Park. We have bought the Sunday papers, it's 25 degrees and I feel that we understand one another. I am talking about Euro 96. Philippa is talking about her visit to Cairo Zoo.

One cage, she said, was marked 'Lions', another 'Giraffes', and a third 'Zebras'. Yet each one contained buffaloes.

'I kept thinking, Now we'll get to see a different animal, but no – every single time it was buffaloes. They seemed to have run out of other species. I felt especially sorry for the buffaloes floating in the aquarium.'

I am instantly struck by the parallel with the mutually indistinguishable teams playing under different country names in Euro 96. Somehow I know not to mention this to Philippa.

'Interesting,' I say. Philippa is pleased that she has said something interesting.

17 June At the chocolate dispenser at work I offer my sympathy to my Scottish colleague Andrew. 'At one point I thought you would win,' I said.

'That's what I thought,' said Andrew. 'But unfortunately we can't score goals. Beforehand you think, Pah! A mere detail, but it turns out to be quite a central element in this sport.'

18 June Today it's England/Holland. In the morning I walk past our foreign news desk.

'Your boys are going down tonight,' says Robert, who is the European news editor.

'4-1,' predicts Richard. Richard is a little 50-year-old man who tried to climb Everest two weeks ago. He failed.

'Are you sure?' I ask.

'Yes,' says Robert. 'But I thought Labour would win the 1983 election, and Richard is still suffering from oxygen deprivation.'

'Excuse me, have you got a ticket for tonight?' asks Richard.

I'm neither English nor Dutch. Really I'm nothing at all. But I spent my childhood in the Netherlands and since then I've supported Holland at football. Tonight I switch sides. Holland are lazy. England play perfect football. Gazza is brilliant. Sheringham is brilliant. Even Pearce and Southgate are not bad. It's as if in a large church in the open air, with 70,000 people watching, a miracle has taken place.

My French colleagues just shake their heads. It's incomprehensible. But when the 4-0 goes in, it turns out that words exist to describe the feeling.

The whole ground is singing:

Football's coming home,
It's coming home, it's coming home.

Even the French are secretly singing along.

In the press centre it emerges that the Dutch are somewhat less moved by events.

'I'm glad they won,' says a journalist from *De Telegraaf* newspaper. 'What else do they have in this awful country? It's all incest here! I think they keep getting more stupid. In 50 years' time they'll be dead of misery.' In support of his case he cites Luton city centre.

The Holland players are also relaxed in defeat. Edwin van der Sar, the goalkeeper, asks the press if today is Tuesday.

David Platt asks an English journalist about the 3.30 at Newmarket.

At 11.30 the Rotterdam journalist Hugo Borst and I reach the tube station. An exceptionally fat woman is jumping up and down at the entrance.

'Well done mate!' she yells at me.

'You also played well!' I shout just as enthusiastically.

For a moment she stops jumping and looks me straight in the eye: 'We beat the fuckers at last!'

In the West End Hugo and I find my Spanish bar, where tonight it is 35 degrees. From his Euro 96 bag, Hugo produces an orange shirt. 'Richard Witschge gave me his Holland shirt after the game,' says Hugo. 'Footballers' shirts always smell of sweat and war. Go on, sell it.'

I smell Witschge's shirt. It smells quite pleasant. There is no trace of sweat.

At four in the morning I get to bed.

19 June   I wake up at eight, slap myself in the face a few times, and write my post-match analysis for Agence France Presse. Then I go to work. As soon as I step out through the front door – drying nicely in the sun – I notice that England has become another country. People are talking to each other on the street. Every now and then someone smiles. It is virtually Africa.

At the platform where I wait for my train there is – as there is every morning – a sign that reads as follows: 'On Saturday 10 January 1863 the Metropolitan Railway Line opened to the public the world's first urban Underground railway. Baker Street was one of the seven original stations.'

The people standing on this platform in 1863 must have thought: 'This is unbelievable. We are the centre of the world.'

Several months later, the rules of modern football were codified in England.

The people standing on the same platform today, with their newspapers full of pictures of England goals, are thinking: 'This is unbelievable. We are – to some extent – the centre of the world again.' They are thinking: 'Maybe the tube will improve now, maybe we'll become richer, maybe the sense that we are sinking into the sea will diminish.'

> *Thirty years of hurt,*
> *Never stopped me dreaming.*

22 June   It's Saturday, I don't have to work, and so I sit on the train to Liverpool for three hours and watch England/Spain on TV in the Anfield press centre with some Spanish journalists.

Then I go to the press box and catch odd moments of Holland losing to France. I spend most of the match trying to repair my modem. This time Asian newspaper readers will have to cope without my insights.

23 June   On my free Sunday I take the train from Liverpool to Manchester to see Germany/Croatia.

In the Old Trafford press centre before the match I discover a table covered with plastic bags. The woman behind the table gives me a bag. It contains a T-shirt; a can of beer; a can of soft drink.

I walk rapidly to my friend Duncan, an American journalist. Duncan is engaged in a difficult conversation with a journalist from the Tokyo *Shimbun*. I announce that plastic bags are being given away free. The Japanese journalist legs it. When he returns he is already wearing the T-shirt. Free! With European letters! It says: 'Manchester Soccer City 96.' There are no more bags left. 'I didn't want one anyway,' says Duncan.

★   ★   ★

The match starts and for once it's not buffalo against buffalo. The Croats are brilliant in phases. Yet Germany get a penalty. As Klinsmann prepares to take it I consider emulating the Cameroonian fan who once ran on to the pitch to clear the ball from his team's goal-line. Klinsmann scores.

Suker equalises. Then Stimac is sent off, and immediately Sammer makes it 2-1. Germany win the match.

I might have known.

Afterwards, the Croats think they should have won. I think so too. I pace furiously through the press centre and try to bump into German journalists. Blazevic, the Croat manager, appears on the TV screen and speaks the mantra of the defeated coach:

> *Their penalty was no penalty.*
> *We should have had a penalty.*
> *Amen.*

The only good thing about the match is that I have found A Moment that Sums Up German Football History. It is this: Ladic, the Croat keeper, is wandering around his penalty area with the ball at his feet. A German striker hurls himself at him. But Ladic feints and shimmies, and the German ends up sprawled over an advertising board 20 yards away. The crowd laughs, and Ladic looks around triumphantly. Suddenly the German is back and this time he almost takes the ball off Ladic!

Even if Germany has been humiliated by a moustachioed goalkeeper, it constantly arises from the ruins, starts at Zero Hour after each setback, and succeeds even when the rest of the world thinks it has no right to.

Naturally this bears no relation to German postwar history.

On the three-hour train trip home I share a hot corridor with an

Indonesian journalist. I ask him who the people back home are supporting.

'They're just hoping that Portugal will be knocked out soon,' he says. Most Indonesians think Portugal is lovely, he reassures me. But due to the dispute over East Timor, Indonesian television is boycotting the Portuguese matches. If Portugal reach the final, the game will not be shown on TV.

24 June   I speak to my mother on the telephone. She says that she and my father, like most other South African Jews in London, are not sure whether to support England or Germany on Wednesday. 'Normally we always hope that England will lose, because the English are unbearable in victory. You can see that now. But of course we also always hope that Germany will lose.'

25 June   Labour's lead in the opinion polls has fallen by six points since England beat Spain. This is the largest Conservative gain in two years. Suppose that England beat Germany tomorrow. In that case they will probably win the final as well. Then the euphoria will continue, Major will call the general election for the early autumn, and he might well win.

26 June   Today is the big day. I note the most important experiences of Germany and England since 1945:

Germany	*England*
Economic miracle	Economy decays
World Cup 1954	Loss of colonies
World Cup 1974	Charles and Di get divorced
World Cup 1990	World Cup 1966

And yet the English don't hate the Germans. Instead, they admire them. Because Germany is the England of the late twentieth century: the strongest, richest country in the world with the best football team. They are just like us, only better. But if we win tonight everything could change. Then we would suddenly be the England of 1966 again. Then we might have 30 years of successes, like Germany.

There's a lot at stake tonight.

Everyone in the office is talking about it. 'It's the repeat of the '66 World Cup final,' says Patrick.

Richard, who looks up stock market prices for us, is a skinhead and a member of the British Communist Party. 'Do you know what Marx would have said?' he asks Patrick.

'That England will win 3-1.'

'Marx would have said: every important historical event occurs twice, the first time as tragedy, the second time as farce.'

'I think it'll be 3-1.'

The bond market closes down for three minutes this afternoon for all traders to join in a rendition of 'Three Lions on a Shirt'.

Jane, my boss, reads my article about a car dealer that has bought another car dealer. It will dwarf the rest of tomorrow's news. Then Motoko, Patrick and I are allowed to leave early, because a PR company has given us tickets to the match.

In the tube people are singing.

> *Who do you think you are kidding Mr Hitler,*
> *If you think old England's done?*

At Wembley 70,000 people are queuing with their tickets. The man in front of me asks the turnstile operator: 'Is this the way to Neasden High Street?'

The PR company turns out to have put us high above the corner flag. The seats are terrible. But three rows behind us are two legendary figures of British postwar history.

'The big man in the raincoat, who is swaying to the rhythm of "Three Lions on a Shirt", is Geoff Hurst,' I explain to Motoko, a Japanese-American woman with Hungarian-Jewish blood. 'In the World Cup final of 1966 he scored three goals. The little man next to him, who looks like a bank clerk, is Martin Peters. Peters scored the other England goal in the match. It's a little bit like sitting three rows in front of Abraham Lincoln and John F. Kennedy.'

Motoko doesn't know what to say.

The match is exciting. The German fans make mad cow noises at the English fans, who respond by making aeroplane gestures and humming the opening bars of 'Dambusters'. Somewhere among them is A.S. Byatt.

England score and Germany score too. Patrick grows increasingly pale. After 70 minutes he says: 'If I was sitting at home I'd leave the room now.'

Our PR host takes things more lightly. 'I'm going to get some drinks,' he says after 80 minutes. 'What do you lot want?'

After 90 minutes it's still 1-1. Patrick says England should bring on Hurst. There are no goals in extra time. The penalties start. The first ten all go in. You're not quite normal if, with 80 million people watching, you can hit your penalty high into the inside of the side netting. Especially not if you are Stuart Pearce.

A tall Englishman – Tony Adams, perhaps? – misses the eleventh penalty. Andy Möller scores from the German penalty.

Patrick looks straight ahead. Motoko's eyes go red. And me? I don't mind. It's a shame that the euphoria of the past eleven days is over. I feel sorry for Patrick and Motoko. But when it comes down to it I'm not English. It was a good game.

The PR people make us go to a Mastercard reception in the Wembley Hilton. There are a hundred people in the room but no one says anything, except for an American behind us who is singing:

> *Football's coming home,*
> *It's coming home,*
> *It's coming home!*

After a while Motoko can speak again. She says it's unfair that a match like this should be decided by penalties. And that she'll never again have the chance to feel English, because in a month's time she's going to become our correspondent in Brazil, and then she'll probably end up in Japan or the States and get married and have kids. In 32 years' time the European Championships will be held in England again and she'll read about it in the *Petaluma Sun* and think, 'When I was 26 I thought that was a big deal.'

'Stay another 30 years,' says Patrick. 'We might reach another semi-final.'

Then the highlights appear on TV. It turns out that it wasn't Adams but Southgate who missed the penalty. And now my eyes almost go red. Southgate, that nice boy with the big nose, will have to carry this burden for the rest of his life.

27 June Southgate has become the national hero. John Major hugged him outside Wembley last night. The newspapers today say he was probably the best player in Euro 96. And why? Because he's a loser. That open, naïve face, the big nose, his admission afterwards that he had been sure he would score – Southgate personifies England.

Germans are efficient people who hit their penalties high into the inside of the side-netting. We are Gareth Southgate. How could we ever have imagined that we would beat the Germans?

★ ★ ★

Today the euphoria has vanished. It's raining and the tube is on strike. 'Clichés,' grumbles one of my colleagues.

Motoko sends me an e-mail asking me to come by her desk quickly. Now she really is upset. The *FT* has told her she can't go to Brazil.

She asks me: 'Do you know the secret of human life?' As it happens I do, but before I can say it Motoko does: 'Life is like a shoot-out against Germany, with Gareth Southgate taking the deciding penalty for you.'

'That's right,' I say. 'There are occasional moments of hope, a high degree of chance, and the certainty that it will all end badly.'

'With hindsight I think penalties were a good way to decide the match,' she says.

Patrick has been thinking too. 'The Germans should have said, "OK, we've won, but you can go to the final. You need it more than we do".'

Patrick says his nephew is a broken child. This is the worst thing that has ever happened to the boy, and he thinks that living on is pointless. But his mother says he was much more upset when Liverpool lost the Cup final last month.

My mother calls.
    'Who did you support?' I ask.
    'Germany.'

29 June   Mickey, an old friend of my grandmother's, supports the Czech Republic. She lived there for 30 years, because she married a Czech soldier in the war.

'Didn't you mind living behind the Iron Curtain for 30 years?' I ask.

'The regime was all right,' she says. 'It was my husband I couldn't stand.'

'The Czechs are doing well, aren't they?' I say.

'And the strange thing is that they're an extraordinarily bad team.'

The *Financial Times* reports that until the semi-final, Czech politicians had been bitterly fighting for seats in the new cabinet. 'But within hours of the victory over France they emerged smiling and waving an agreement that had eluded them for more than a month.'

Philippa can't make it again tonight, but fortunately I have another date. The German team is staying 300 yards from my front door, in the Landmark Hotel. I walk past the Allsop Arms and the local tramps, who are wearing discarded England caps and scarves, and turn into the Marylebone Road. At the Landmark I have arranged to meet Helmut Klopfleisch.

I know Klopfleisch from a year I once spent in Berlin. He is a moon-faced electrician who was born in East Berlin in 1948 and became a Hertha BSC fan shortly afterwards. But on 13 August 1961 the Berlin Wall went up. For a while Klopfleisch spent every Saturday afternoon huddled beside the Wall with other Hertha fans, listening to the sounds from the stadium a few hundred yards away in the West. The border guards soon put a stop to this.

For the next 28 years Klopfleisch followed western football teams around Eastern Europe. The Stasi, the East German secret police, noticed. Klopfleisch was often arrested – in 1986 for instance, for sending a good-luck telegram to the West German team at the World Cup in Mexico. 'How dare you wish the Class Enemy good luck?' the Stasi had asked him.

He was expelled from the GDR in 1989, months before the Wall came down. Since then he has followed the German national team around the world. He has become the unofficial team mascot, licensed to hang around in the hotel and chat to players.

This evening he is sitting at a table in the lobby of the Landmark with the president of Werder Bremen and an old man in check trousers. Fritz Scherer, the former president of Bayern Munich, is with them, but excuses himself as soon as I arrive. The old man in check trousers is tall and tanned, with elegant grey hair and a perfectly buttoned shirt. It is immediately obvious from his aura that he is a Legend.

When we are introduced I fail to catch his name, and so I guess that he is Fritz Walter, captain of the German team that won the 1954 World Cup. But after a couple of minutes I realise that this man is Bernd Trautmann, 'Bert' to the English. Trautmann is a former POW and the Manchester City goalkeeper said to have broken his neck in an FA Cup final. Of course he didn't break his neck, but he did play on after a spine injury and City won the match. He is a legend.

Trautmann talks like a legend, slowly and ponderously, knowing that whatever he says people will listen. It is a manner common among very beautiful women.

The conversation turns to Nelson Mandela. Trautmann coughs, and we all fall silent. 'I have ordered Mandela's book,' says Trautmann. 'In my house in Spain I have 2,000 books, and I have read most of them. When I come home,' and he looks around our little circle, 'I will read that book.' With great formality he takes a handful of nuts from the bowl on the table.

This goes on for a couple of hours. And yet I find it interesting. First of all, Trautmann is indeed a legend, so that nothing he says is dull. But also, the atmosphere here is calm and soothing. I assume that this is typical of team camps where everything is going well. The Werder president and Trautmann occasionally order rounds of beer, nobody looks around to see if they can see anyone more interesting (Jürgen Klinsmann, for instance), and every speaker is permitted time to hold forth.

Klopfleisch alone says little. The general opinion – which I think he shares – is that as a simple electrician he should be grateful to be here at all.

When Trautmann doesn't have anything left to say the Werder president explains to me why the German camp is so calm this tournament: the Bayern players are behaving themselves. It was different in the past, he assures me. He can say that because his good friend Fritz Scherer has left. 'Uli Hoeness, that's the arrogance of Bayern in one man,' says the Werder president.

'Paul Breitner,' says Trautmann. The Werder president shivers as if he has food poisoning.

The Werder players are very serious characters, he says. Sometimes there'll be a talk on religion in town, and a group of them will go along. Not the Jehovah's Witnesses or anything like that. No, serious theology evenings. Not really Bayern's thing, he thinks. The Werder president says that Werder and Bayern represent the two sides of the German character.

'North and south,' I say.

'I'm afraid I must correct you,' he says. 'Werder is the Germany of the collective. No stars. Everyone works hard to build something together. The Germany of the 1950s, as it were.'

'And Bayern?'

'Bayern is the Germany of today. Too rich, spoiled, always quarrelling, and disliked everywhere. And yet they usually win.' And so we come to the great question. Why do Germans always win? Surely these men should know?

Trautmann takes some more nuts. Klopfleisch and the Werder president look polite but uncomprehending. They don't quite see my point. After all, Germany don't always win. They didn't win the last World Cup, nor any of the last three European Championships. No, things are not going well for

Germany at the moment. The new generation doesn't want to work, and . . .

I give up.

Have they had a nice time in England?

Oh yes. They are all Anglophiles. This country has an air of peace that Germany lacks.

'You know,' says the Werder president, 'I grew up in East Berlin. Later I fled to the West. So the division of Germany determined my life. For Herr Klopfleisch, of course, it was the same. And Herr Trautmann became a Legend as a result of being taken prisoner in the war. But in England nothing has changed for a hundred years. It's the old world. I like that so much. The war put an end to all that in Germany.'

I learned one thing in my time in Berlin: when it gets late and there is beer on the table and a foreigner present, German conversations always turn to the war.

'I am a simple man,' says Trautmann. He pauses. 'This is what I have always remained, but I read my books, and what I read is this: the French, the Americans, the English, they all knew exactly what Hitler was going to do. And so as a simple man I ask myself: Why didn't they do anything? If France had chased him out of the Rhineland in 1936 . . .'

At eleven o'clock he goes to bed. The Werder president follows, but first he puts the beer on his room bill. It's easy when the German football federation is paying, but still.

Klopfleisch and I have a final cup of coffee. 'It's always the same with those old Germans,' says Klopfleisch. 'If this, if that, then Hitler would never have happened and they could sleep easily at night. The German doesn't want to know anything about it. One has to say it: at bottom, the German is an arsehole.'

Klopfleisch is bitter. The lives of these three men may have been determined by Hitler, but only Klopfleisch's life was ruined. He was not allowed to go to university, and when he was kicked out of the GDR he lost everything he had. He's pleased that he can go to a tournament in the West with the national team, he says, but it means less to him than it would have in the days of the Wall.

Klopfleisch's complaints are starting to bore me. At bottom, he's a loser. The Legend has gone to bed. I leave as well. 'Good luck tomorrow,' I say, as if Germany needs it.

30 June   It's the final today.

England aren't playing, but the Germans and Czechs do have to shake our Queen's hand. She is wearing a green anorak. The crowd is pleased that she is here. No one else has such a famous queen.

The Czech team are not as bad as Mickey said. But both teams stick rigidly to the UEFA rule forbidding goals in the first half.

After half-time the Czechs take the lead, but then Germany arises from the ruins again. When Bierhoff scores the winning goal almost the entire stadium jeers.

We get another, better, free shoulder bag. Euro 96 is over. I arrive home at last.

Philippa hasn't called in two weeks, I haven't slept for three weeks, I have drunk a lot, eaten a lot of hamburgers, and not washed myself very often. I look several years older than I did on 8 June. I resolve never to leave the house again.

I call Philippa. 'You haven't called for a fortnight,' I say.

'No,' she says.

I don't know what else to say. We agree to meet on Wednesday for a farewell drink.

I get into the bath, the water goes very grey, and through the open window I can hear the German fans serenading their players outside the Landmark Hotel. Moving, isn't it?

★ ★ ★

1 July   Today Gazza, dressed in a bright white suit, is marrying Sheryl. Everyone is charmed and says it is like Charles and Diana's wedding.

3 July   Philippa and I are sitting side by side in a pub, drinking our farewell drinks. I don't say much about Euro 96.

'You know,' I say after two hours (we have drunk a lot of farewell drinks), 'I must say I think it's a bit of a shame that things didn't work out between us.'

Philippa drinks another farewell drink. I quickly start talking about Gareth Southgate again.

'It is,' she says, 'indeed perhaps just a little bit sad.'

I shut up about Southgate. 'Say,' I say, 'that Euro 96 hadn't happened. Do you think things might have worked out then?'

'Well,' she says, 'maybe.'

I fetch two more farewell drinks. She kisses me. I kiss her. This goes on for some time, but I took no notes and therefore can't go into detail.

Everything is very beautiful.

Strangely enough, I never saw her again after that.

the contributors

A BBC poll once declared *Dannie Abse* to be the most popular living British poet. He has published eleven books of poetry and seen several hundred Cardiff City matches.

Hugo Borst is proof that some Dutch football writers are as good as some Dutch footballers. Hugo is the same age as Marco van Basten, and they have been known to hit the town together.

Jimmy Burns was born in Madrid. His first book, *The Land That Lost Its Heroes*, about Argentina and the Falklands War, was praised by Graham Greene. His latest, a biography of Diego Maradona called *Hand of God*, was praised by Noel Gallagher. Jimmy is a Somerset Maugham Prize winner and writes for the *Financial Times*.

Simon Kuper is a *Financial Times* journalist and author of *Football Against the Enemy*, a kind of travel book about football around the world. It won the William Hill Sports Book of the Year prize in 1994.

Emma Lindsey writes for the *Observer* in a manner quite unlike that of any other British sports journalist.

Karl Miller founded and edited the *London Review of Books*, in which he once wrote a legendary paragraph about Paul Gascoigne.

D.J. Taylor's latest work, *The English Settlement*, is that rare thing, a good novel set in a soccer club. Taylor, who was first taken to Carrow Road in 1960 at the age of six weeks, is currently writing a biography of Thackeray. His forthcoming collection of short stories, *After Bathing at Baxter's*, includes 'Fantasy Finals'.

Jorge Valdano scored a goal for Argentina in the 1986 World Cup final. He writes for *El Pais* and is manager of Valencia.

Simon Veksner worked as a merchant banker for Credit Suisse First Boston, as a journalist for the *Evening Standard*, and as a copywriter for Saatchi & Saatchi and now for The Leisure Process. He is 29 and has just completed his first novel, *Class A*.

If Eric Cantona was the creator of the 1990s Manchester United side, *Jim White* is its chronicler. He writes mainly for the *Guardian*.

James Wilson is at home in both Newcastle and Colombia, and he can write. Who better to send in search of Faustino Asprilla? James is 27 and another *Financial Times* journalist.

perfect pitch

2) foreign field

EDITED BY SIMON KUPER

will be published on 7 May 1998 (ISBN 0 7472 7697 8)
in Review softback, on a theme to tie in with the World Cup.
Among those who will be writing for this second edition are:

Patrick Barclay
Ian Buruma
Simon Kuper
D.J. Taylor
Lynne Truss

Further contributors will follow.